Dreadful Ed
&
Mary Scary

DREADFUL ED & MARY SCARY

written by ANDREW COSBY

illustrated by TROY NIXEY

color for *Dreadful Ed* by DAVE STEWART

color for *Mary Scary* by JEROMY COX

cover by TROY NIXEY and DAVE STEWART

DARK HORSE BOOKS™

To Charlie and Kenzie, my favorite little nightmares.—Andrew Cosby

For the six-year-old me—he would have loved this!—Troy Nixey

President & Publisher MIKE RICHARDSON

Collection Editor DANIEL CHABON   Original Editor SHAWNA GORE

Assistant Editors CHUCK HOWITT, JEMIAH JEFFERSON

Designer PATRICK SATTERFIELD   Digital Art Technician ALLYSON HALLER

Published by
DARK HORSE BOOKS
A division of Dark Horse Comics LLC
10956 SE Main Street • Milwaukie, OR 97222

DarkHorse.com

To find a comics shop in your area, visit comicshoplocator.com

First edition: February 2020 | ISBN: 978-1-50671-330-4

1 3 5 7 9 10 8 6 4 2
Printed in China

Library of Congress Cataloging-in-Publication Data

Names: Cosby, Andrew (Television writer), author. | Nixey, Troy,
   illustrator. | Stewart, Dave, colourist, cover artist. | Cox, Jeromy,
   colourist. | Cosby, Andrew (Television writer) Dreadful Ed. | Cosby,
   Andrew (Television writer) Mary Scary.
Title: Dreadful Ed and Mary Scary / written by Andrew Cosby ; illustrated
   by Troy Nixey ; color for Dreadful Ed by Dave Stewart ; color for Mary
   Scary by Jeromy Cox ; cover by Troy Nixey and Dave Stewart.
Description: First edition. | Milwaukie, OR : Dark Horse Books, a division
   of Dark Horse Comics LLC, 2020. | "Collects previously published books
   Dreadful Ed and Mary Scary." | Audience: Ages 12. | Audience: Grades
   7-9. | Summary: In the first story, Ed is sent to fright school to
   prepare to take over for his father, the Boogeyman, but what he learns
   there is a shocking secret about himself. In the second story, Mary
   meets Ed and learns why she has always been so different from her peers.
Identifiers: LCCN 2019037659 | ISBN 9781506713304 (hardcover) | ISBN
   9781506717548 (ebook)
Subjects: LCSH: Graphic novels. | CYAC: Graphic novels. | Schools--Fiction.
   | Secrets--Fiction. | Identity--Fiction. | Monsters--Fiction.
Classification: LCC PZ7.7.C674 Dre 2020 | DDC 741.5/973--dc23
LC record available at https://lccn.loc.gov/2019037659

CHAPTER ONE

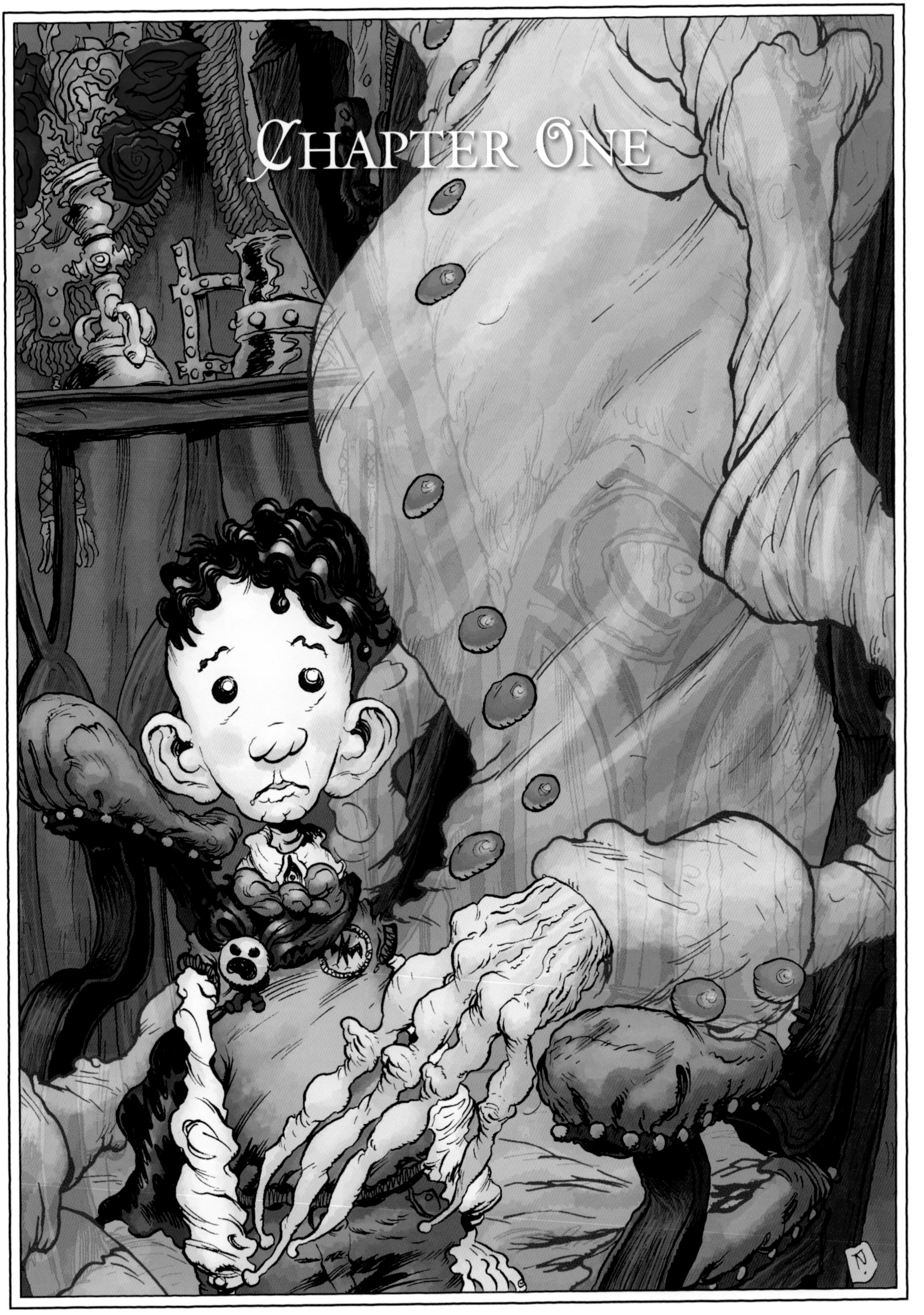

It's a little known fact among those in the know
that on one night each year when the howling winds blow
if you stay up past bedtime 'til thirteen past three
there's a place not like this place you're likely to see.

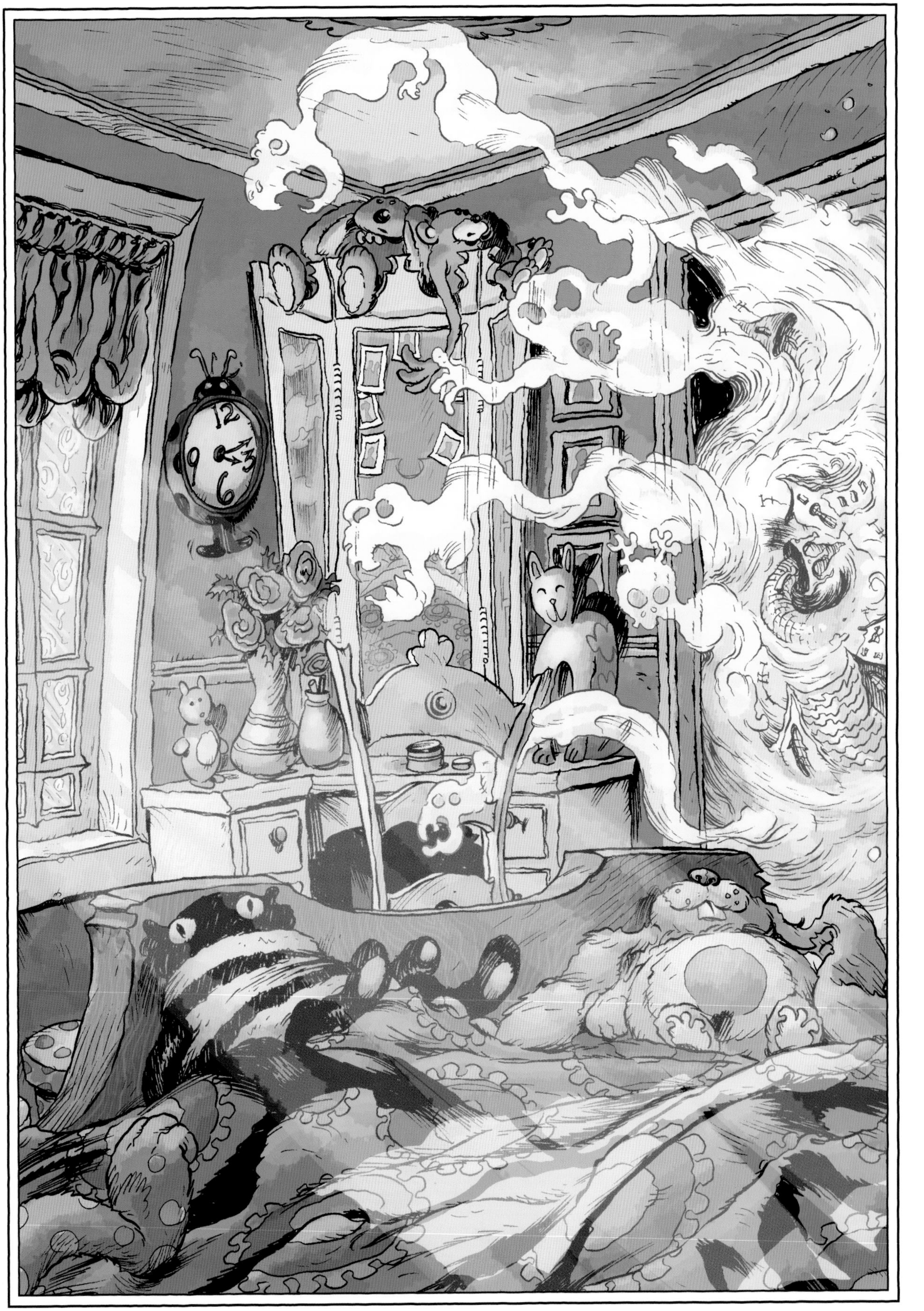

The world of Nocturnia where sleepy things roam,
where shadows and nightmares and monsters call home.
Where up can be down and wrong's often right.
A land full of wonder and thunder and fright.

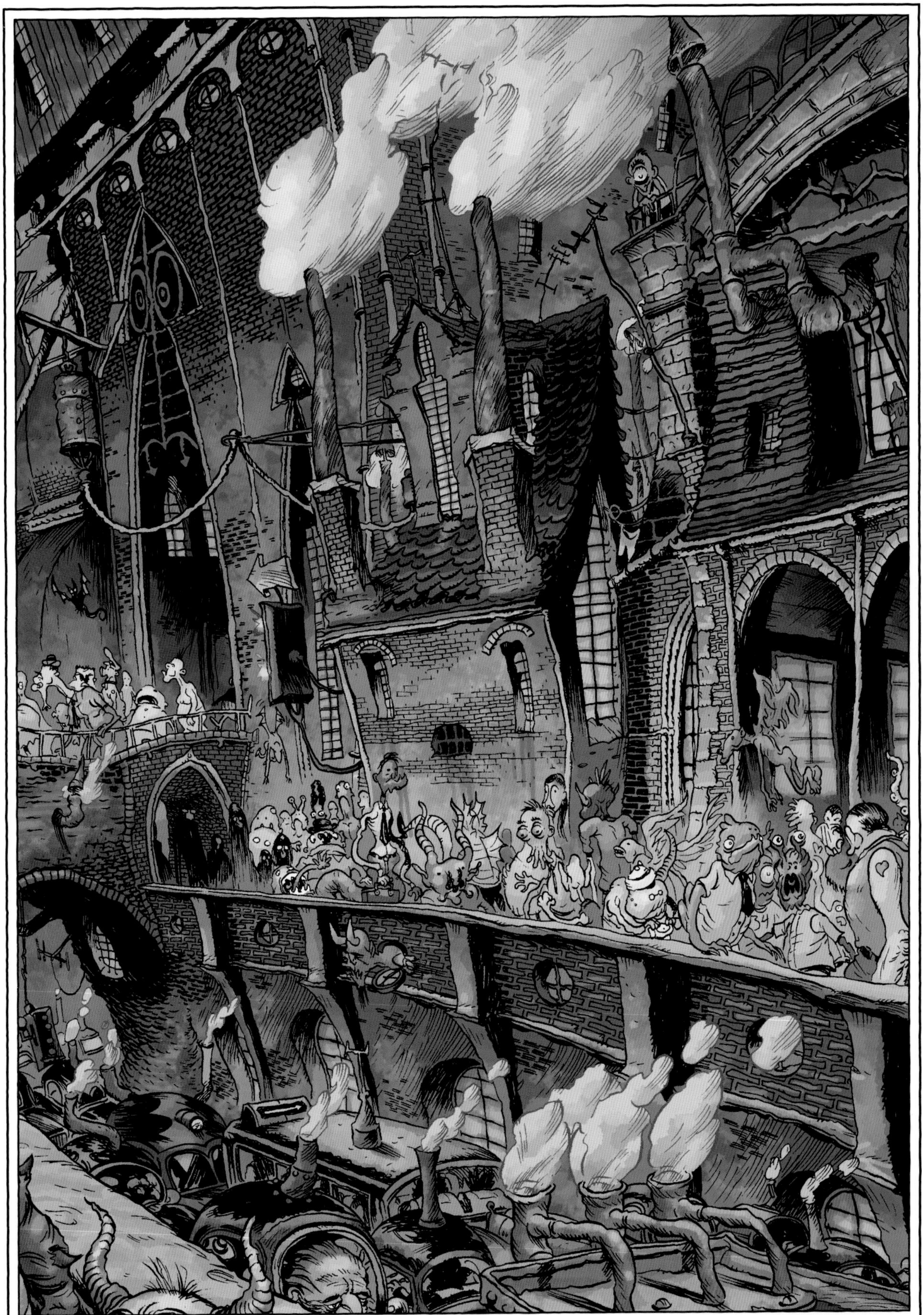

With gleaming black towers as tall as the sky
and ghostly grey gasses that go wafting by
it's in this dark dreamscape our story begins,
with the Boogeyman, wife, and their six sets of twins . . .

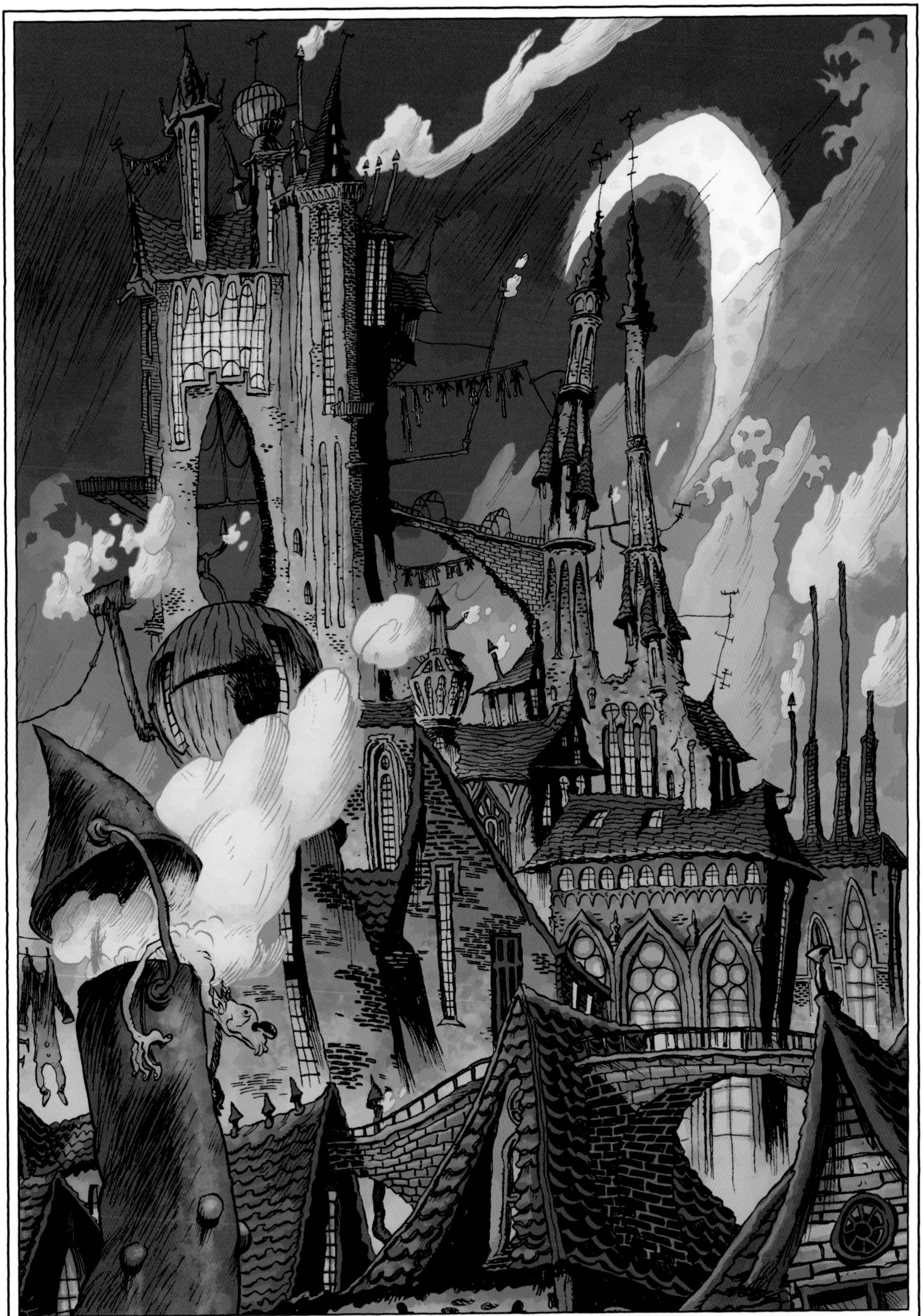

It happened one evening while sitting to dine.
Boogey noticed Lenore had not touched her wine.
Though quite hard to tell from where he was sitting,
it looked very much like Lenore might be knitting . . .

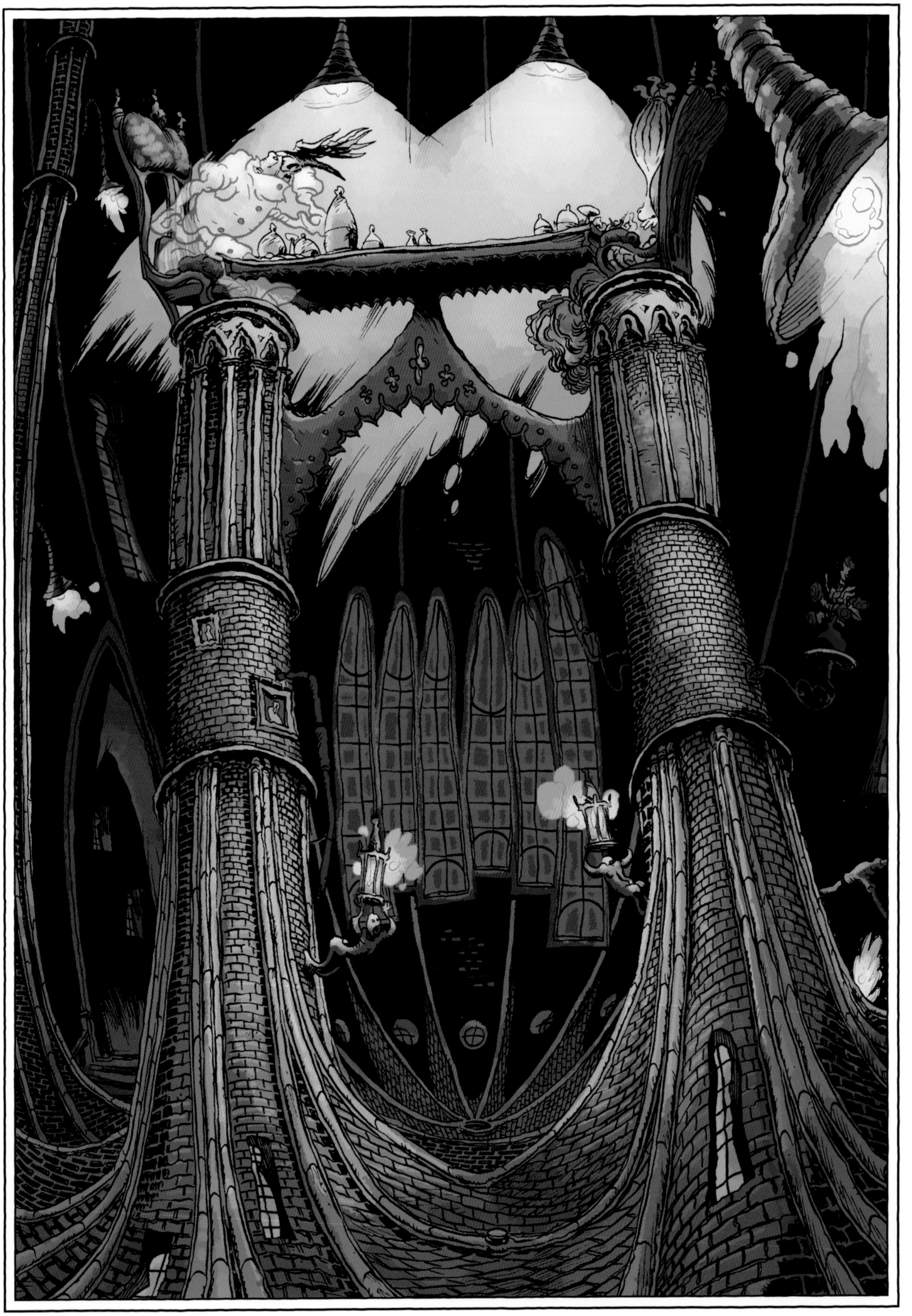

"What's that, my dear?" the Boogeyman cried.
"Why nothing, my love," she promptly replied.
But Boogey knew better, the signs were all there.
"You're knitting booties! Have I got an HEIR?"

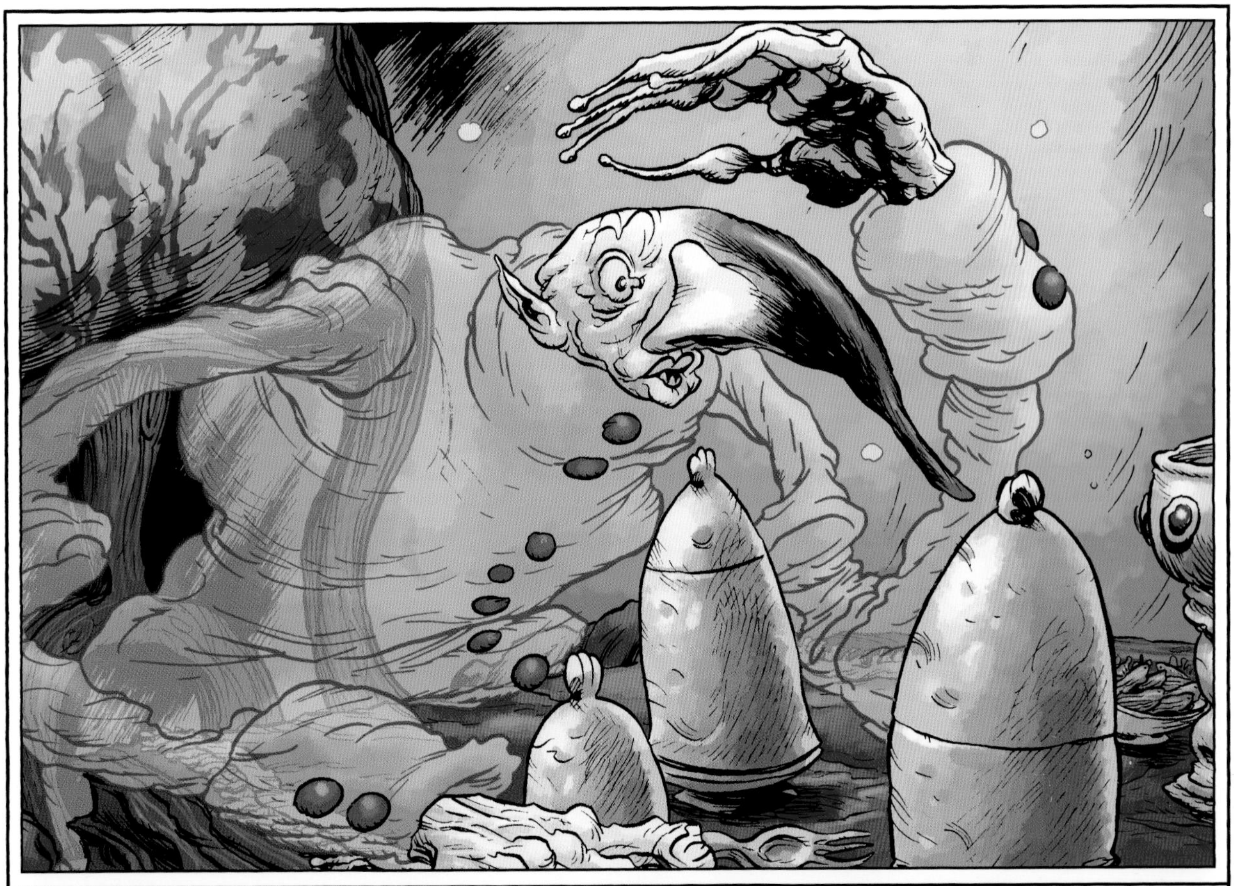
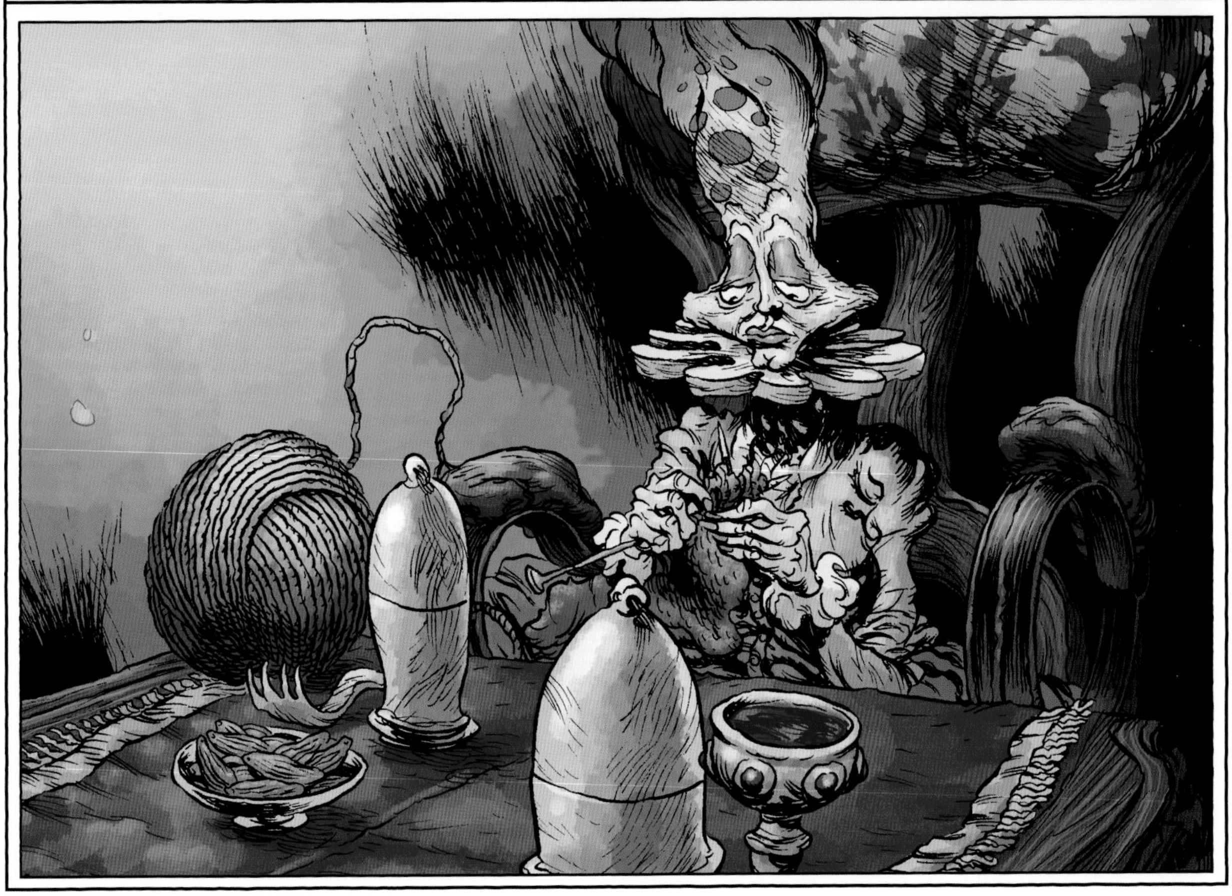

Yes, it was true. Lenore was with child.
And with that reveal, the Boogey went wild,
his little black heart near bursting with joy,
for he had only daughters and was expecting a boy.

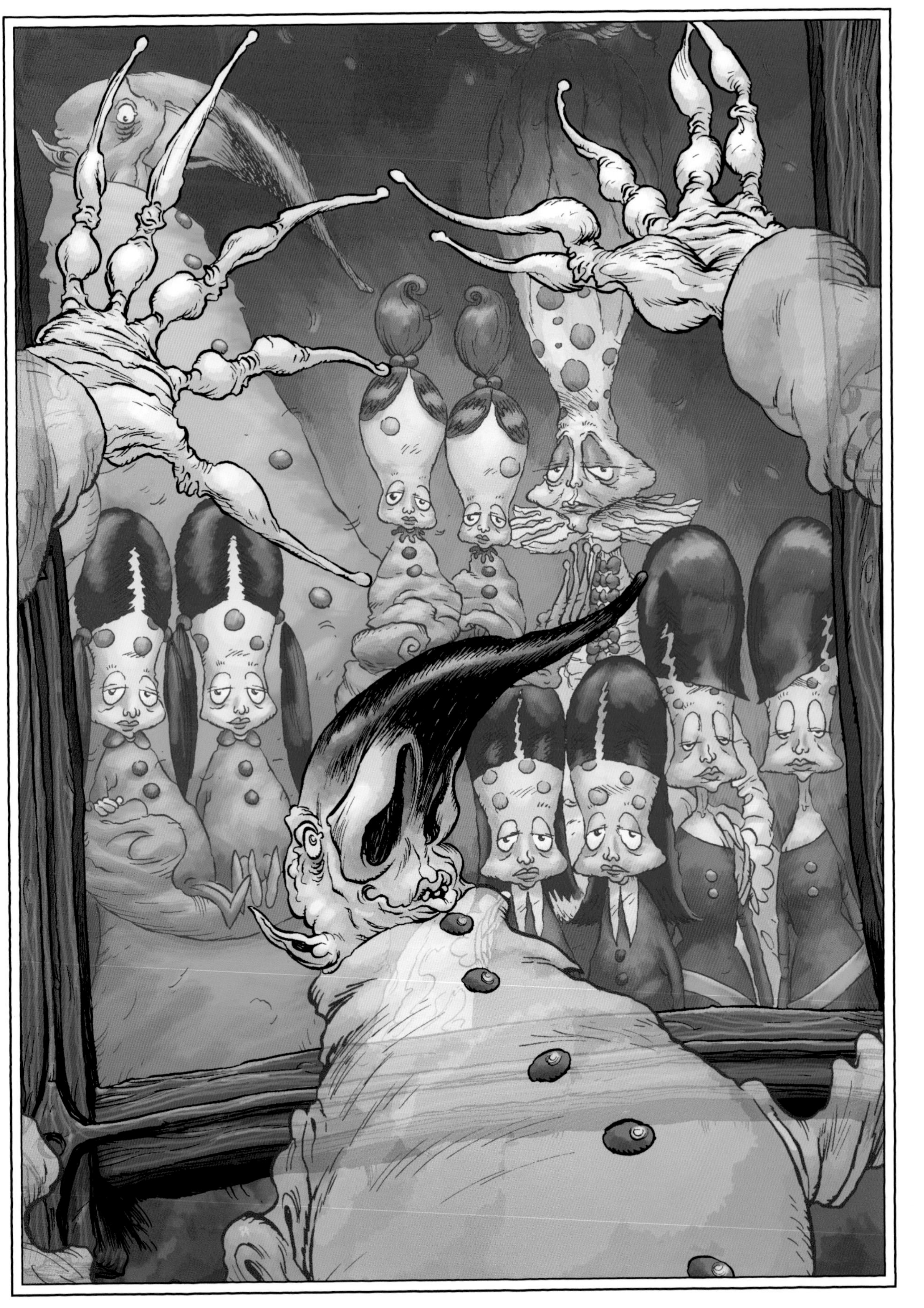

At last, there is someone to carry my name!
A Boogeyman junior to teach the fright game.
Now I can retire and with no reservation
as sire to a son who deserves my vocation."

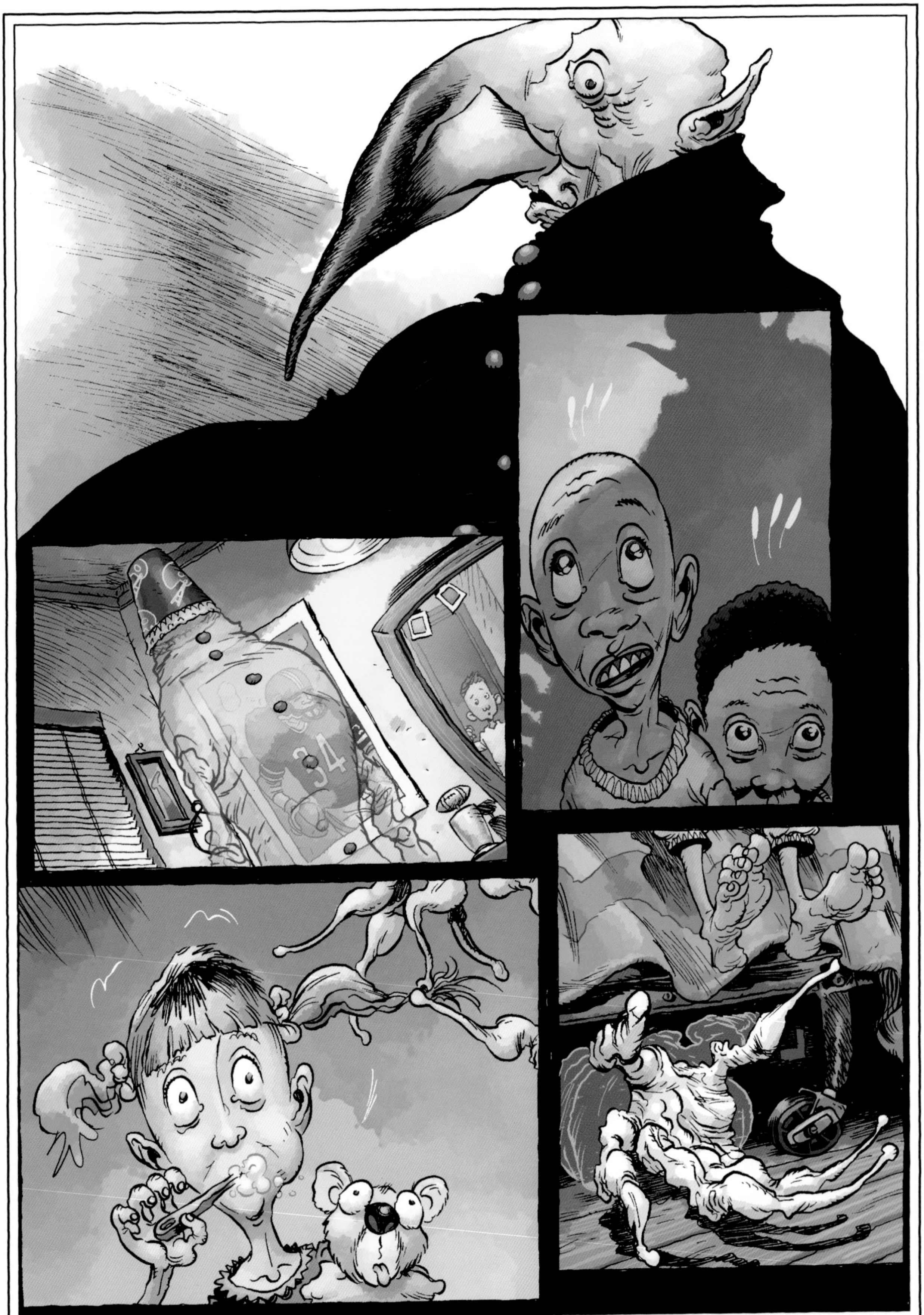

And so Boogey danced like a new father should,
or like anyone dances when news is this good.

But Lenore wasn't dancing, not a twist, not a twirl.

For she knew in her heart that this boy . . . was a girl.

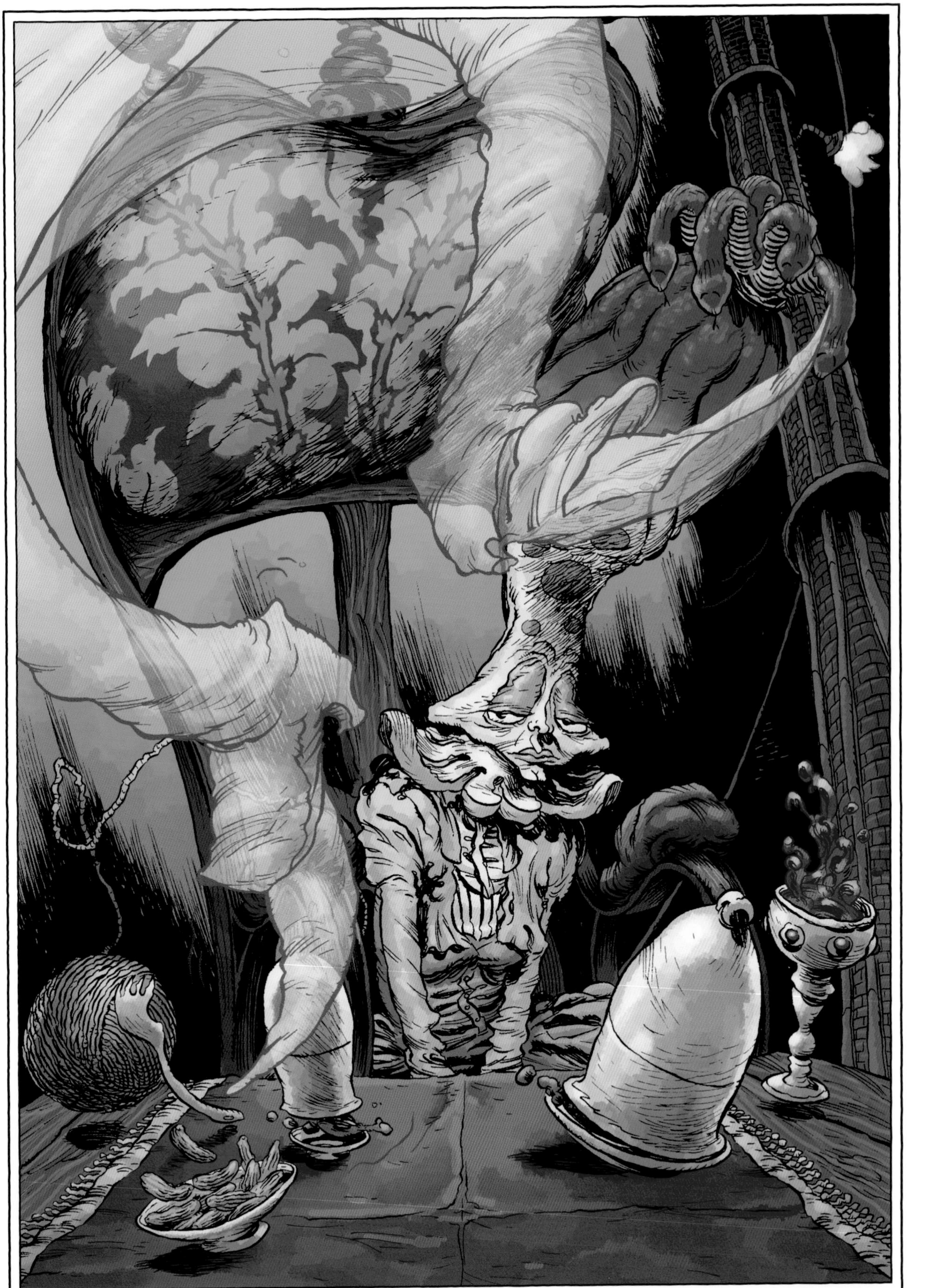

Thirteen months later, Lenore was proved right.

She snatched up her daughter, fled into the night.

A boy he must have, so a boy it must be.

And she knew where to find one . . . come thirteen past three.

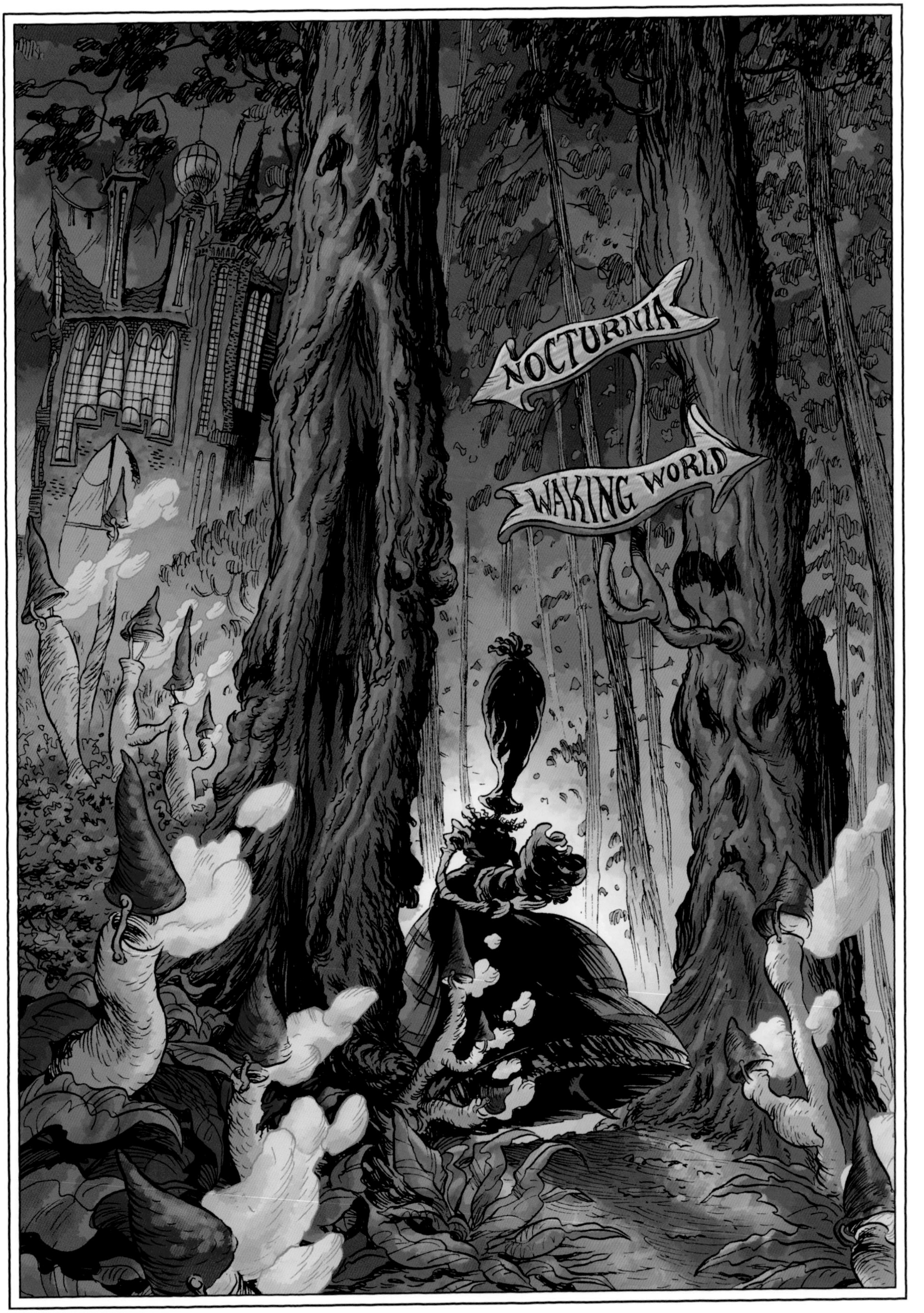
NOCTURNIA
WAKING WORLD

At a Waking World orphanage where children were kept,
she picked the best one while the others all slept.
Lenore said farewell and then sadly smiled,
swapping her girl for a human male child.

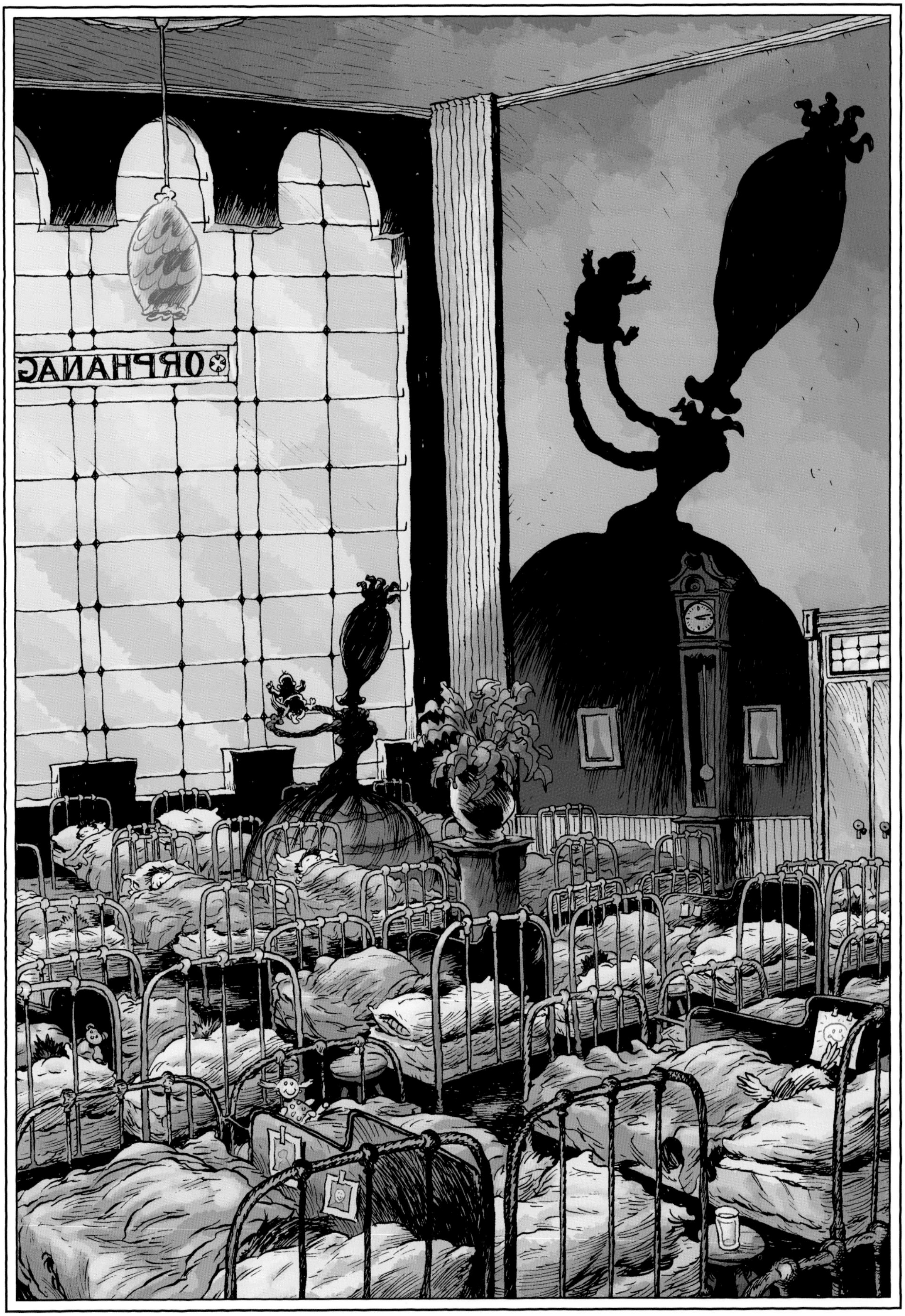
ORPHANAG

They called the boy Edgar, a right proper name
for a Boogeyman prince who was destined for fame.
The nightmares all gathered to give their best wishes
while Boogey stood by, looking on quite suspicious.

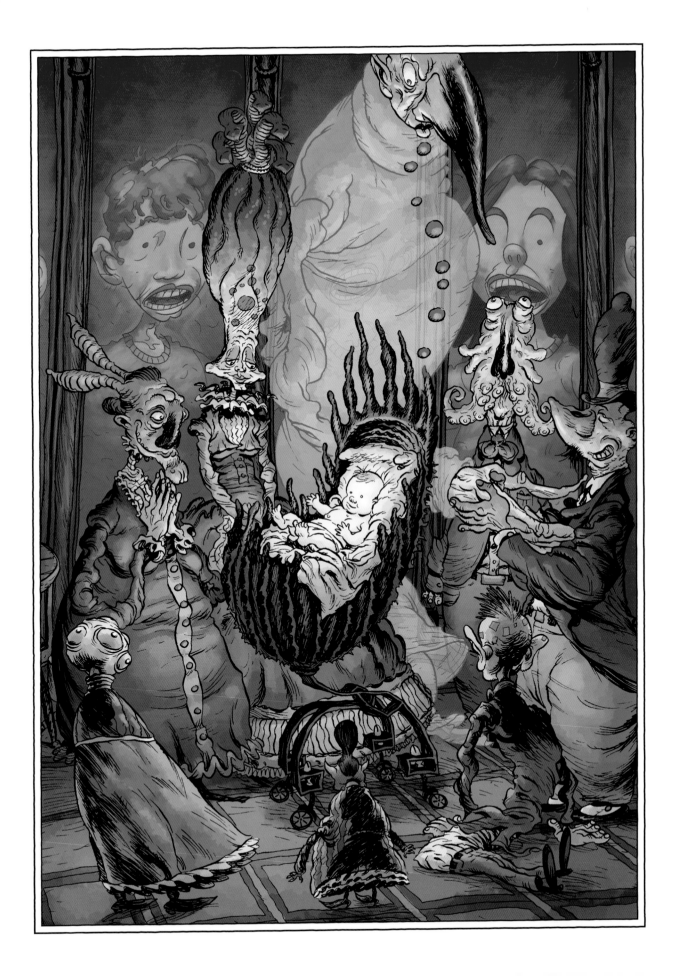

With each passing year, it became rather clear
that young Edgar would never be someone to fear.
He just wasn't like other monsters, you see.
Ed was human. And that's all that he'd ever be.

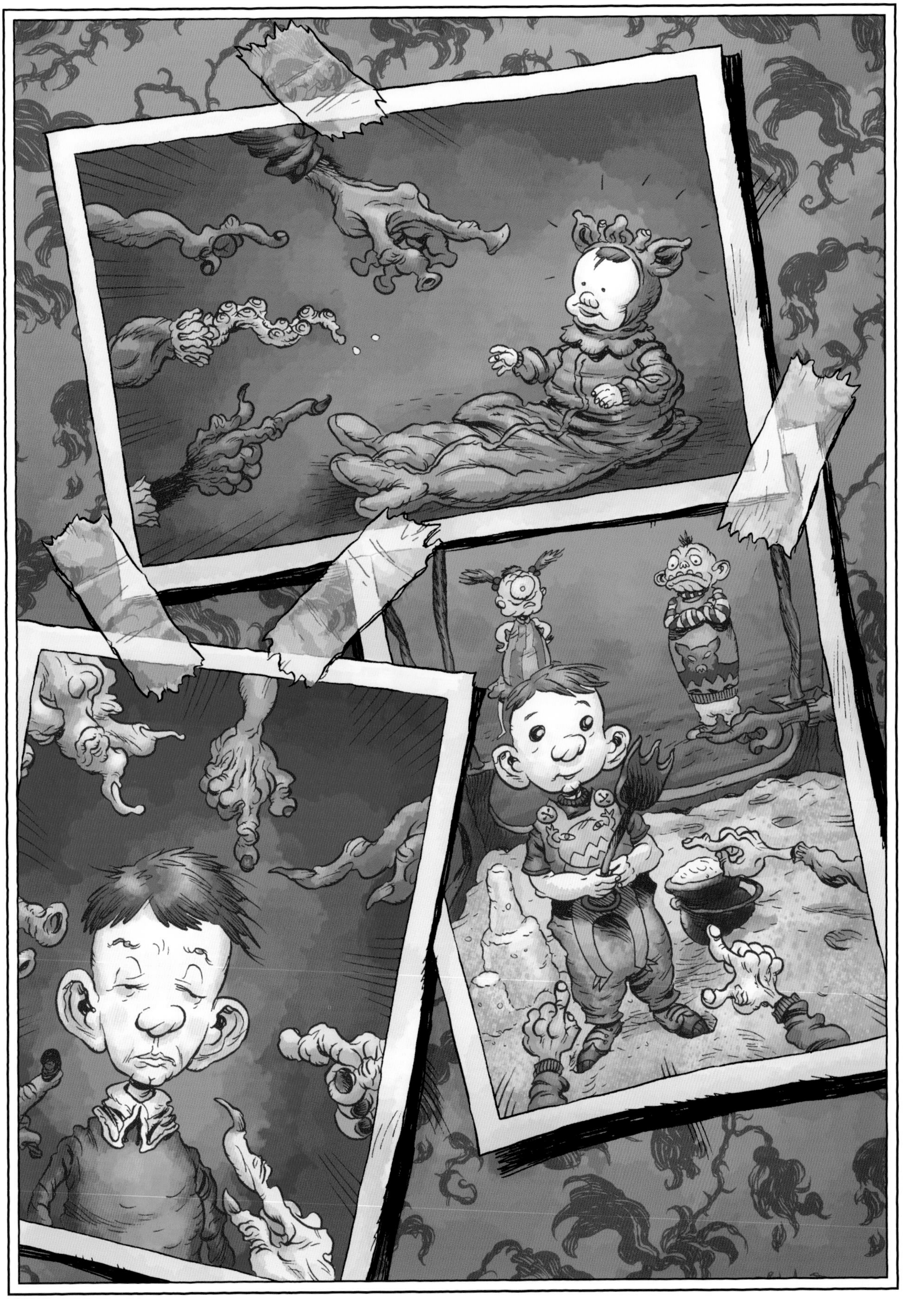

Lenore did her part, dressed him up not so nice,
combed his hair full of squid ink, and shared this advice:
"To be fearsome my dearsome, there's nothing much to it.
Just think of what pleases . . . and then do not do it."

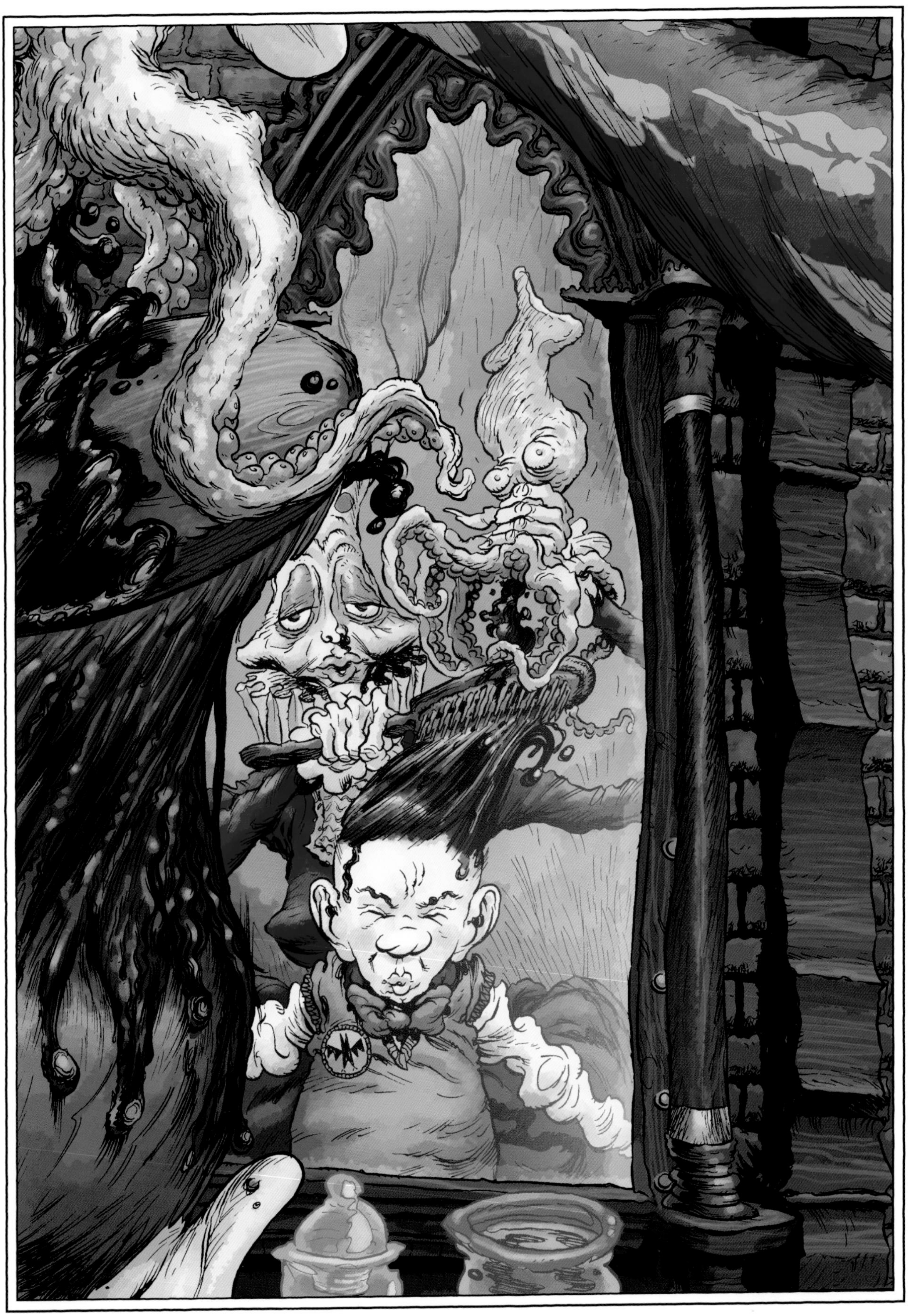

On the first day of Fright School, Ed felt out of place
and knew in an instant he'd be a disgrace.
Surrounded by monsters who all looked chagrined,
Ed wondered if somewhere he might find a friend.

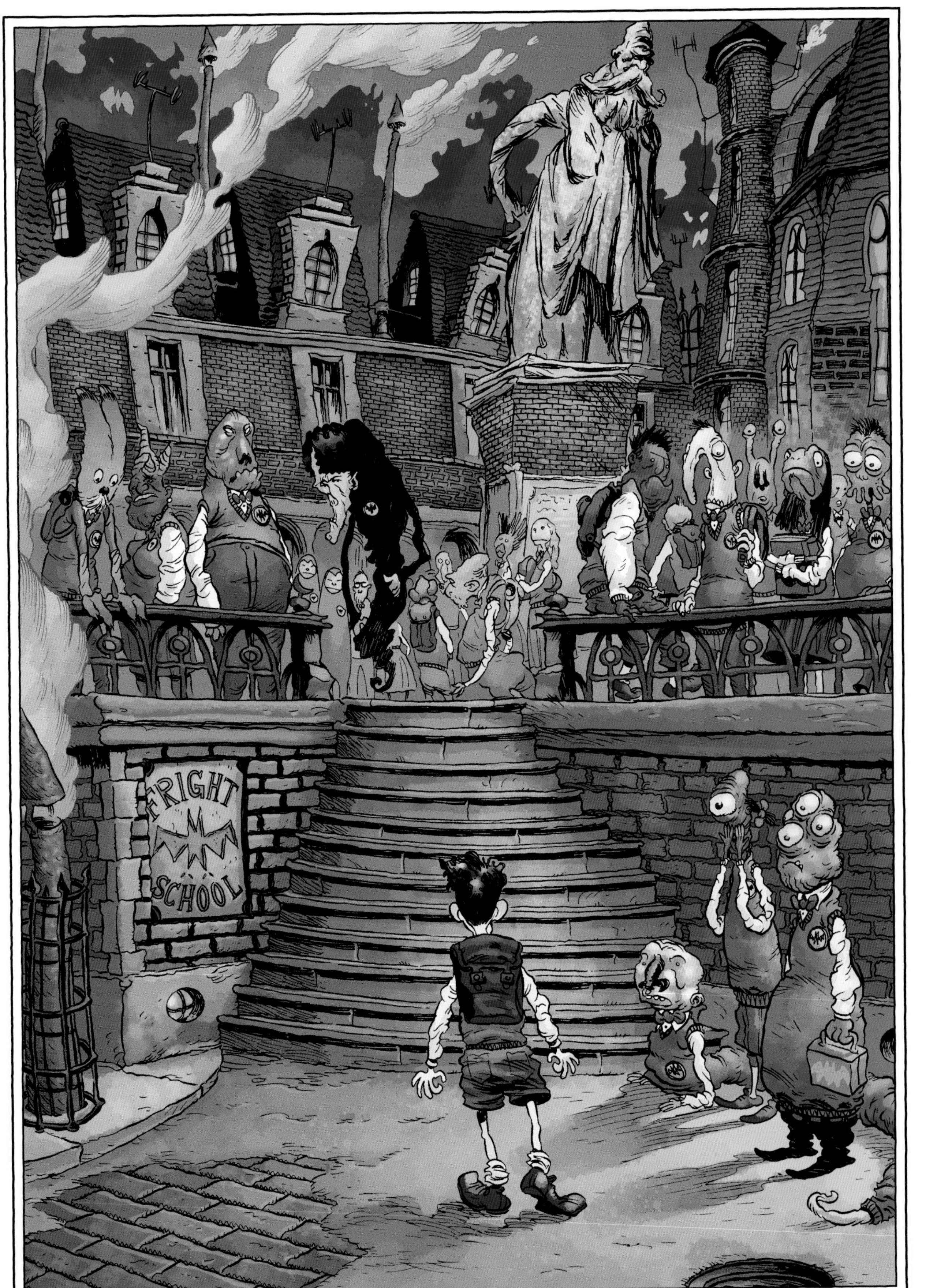
FRIGHT SCHOOL

Although it seemed hopeless, soon Edgar would find
that he wasn't the only young misfit maligned.
There was cute little Hagatha and her little cat Asa,
who lived in the hat perched atop her cabeza.

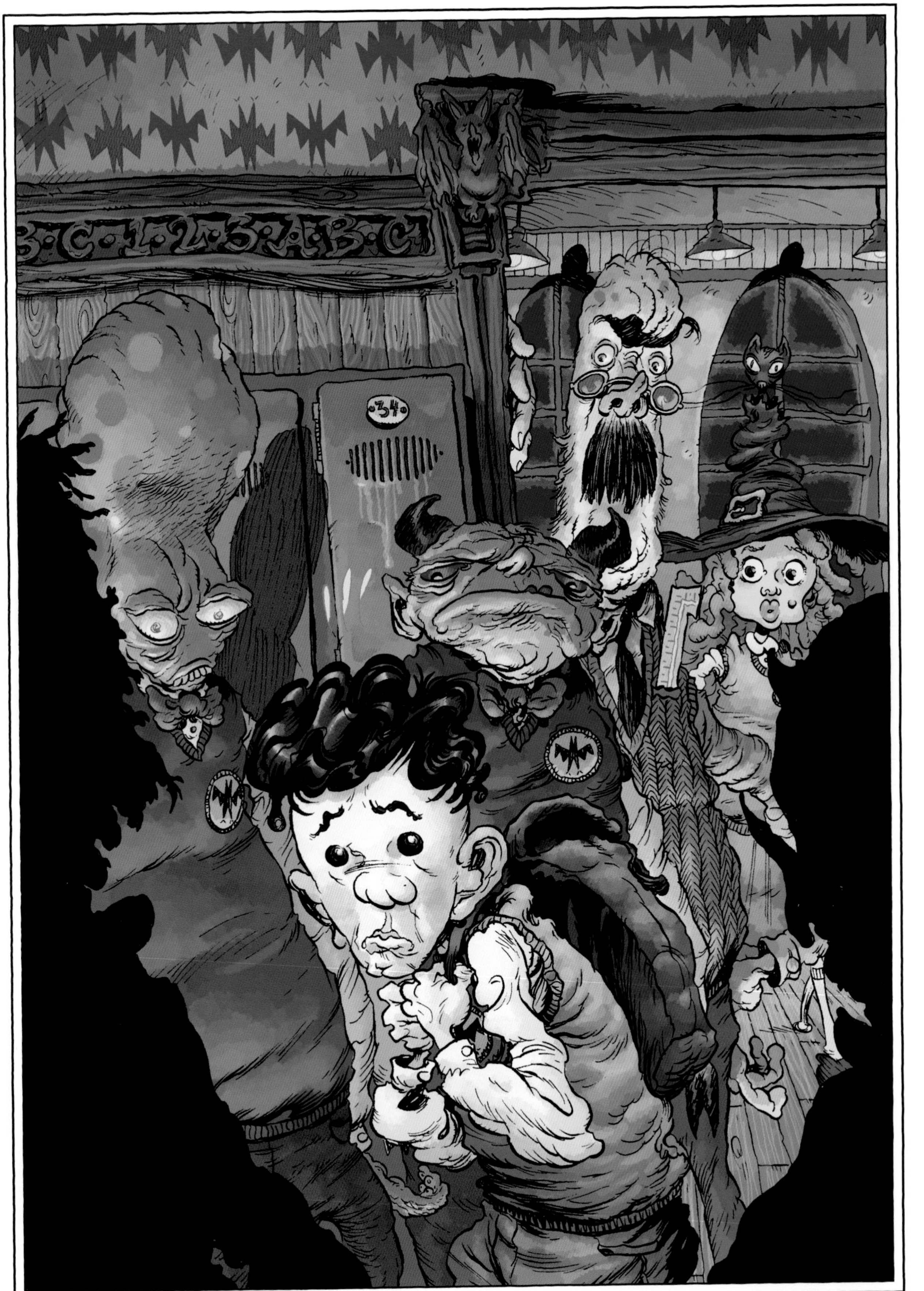
34

And Harry the werewolf who just won't eat meat.

The vampire, Fred—he's undead but still sweet.

A fat little skeleton watching his weight.

A mismatch of monsters to share Edgar's fate.

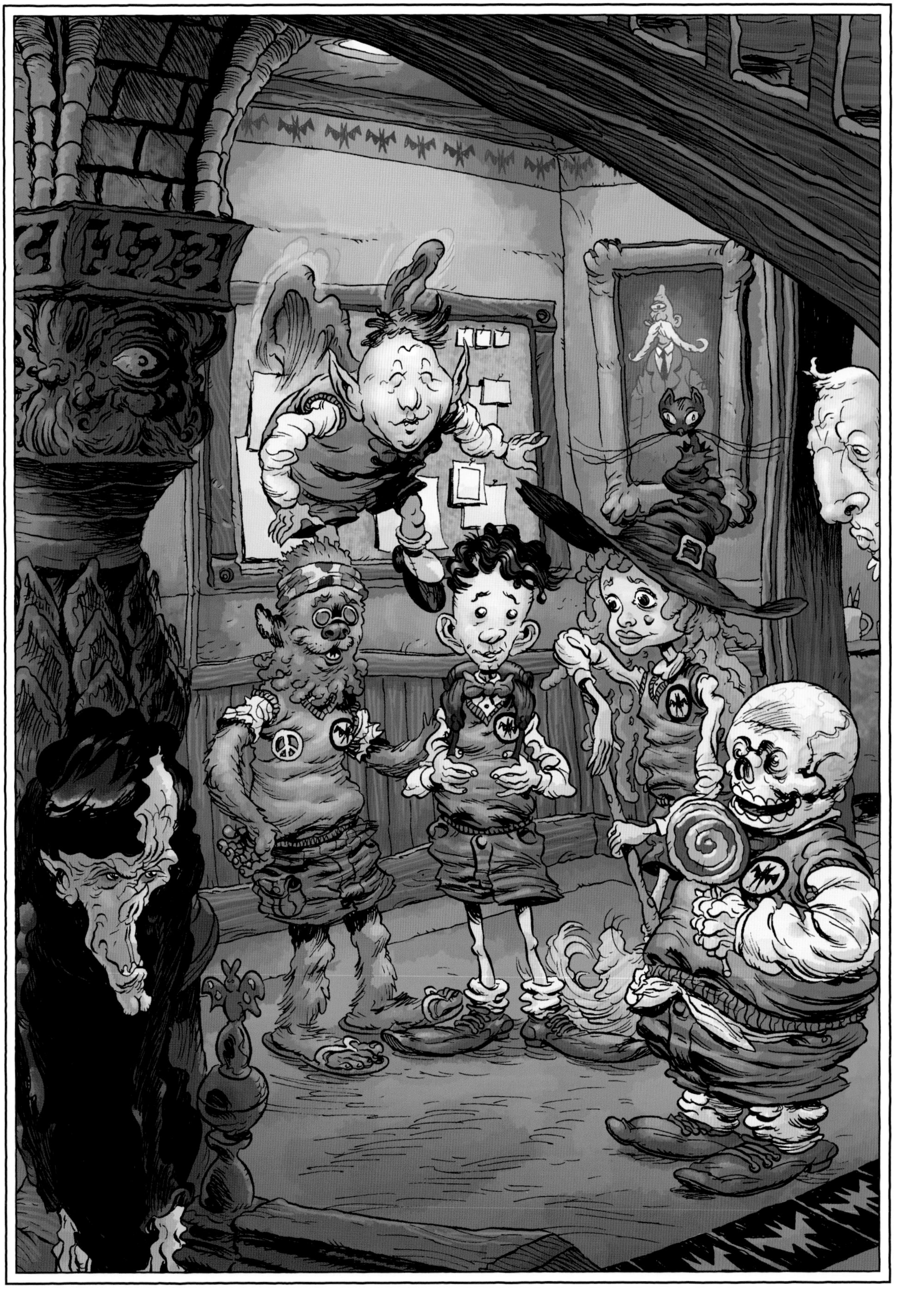

But despite his new friends, Ed still didn't fit in.

No claws, horns, or fangs . . . not even a fin.

His grades were abysmal, and his teachers were wary

that Ed would forever be more scared than scary.

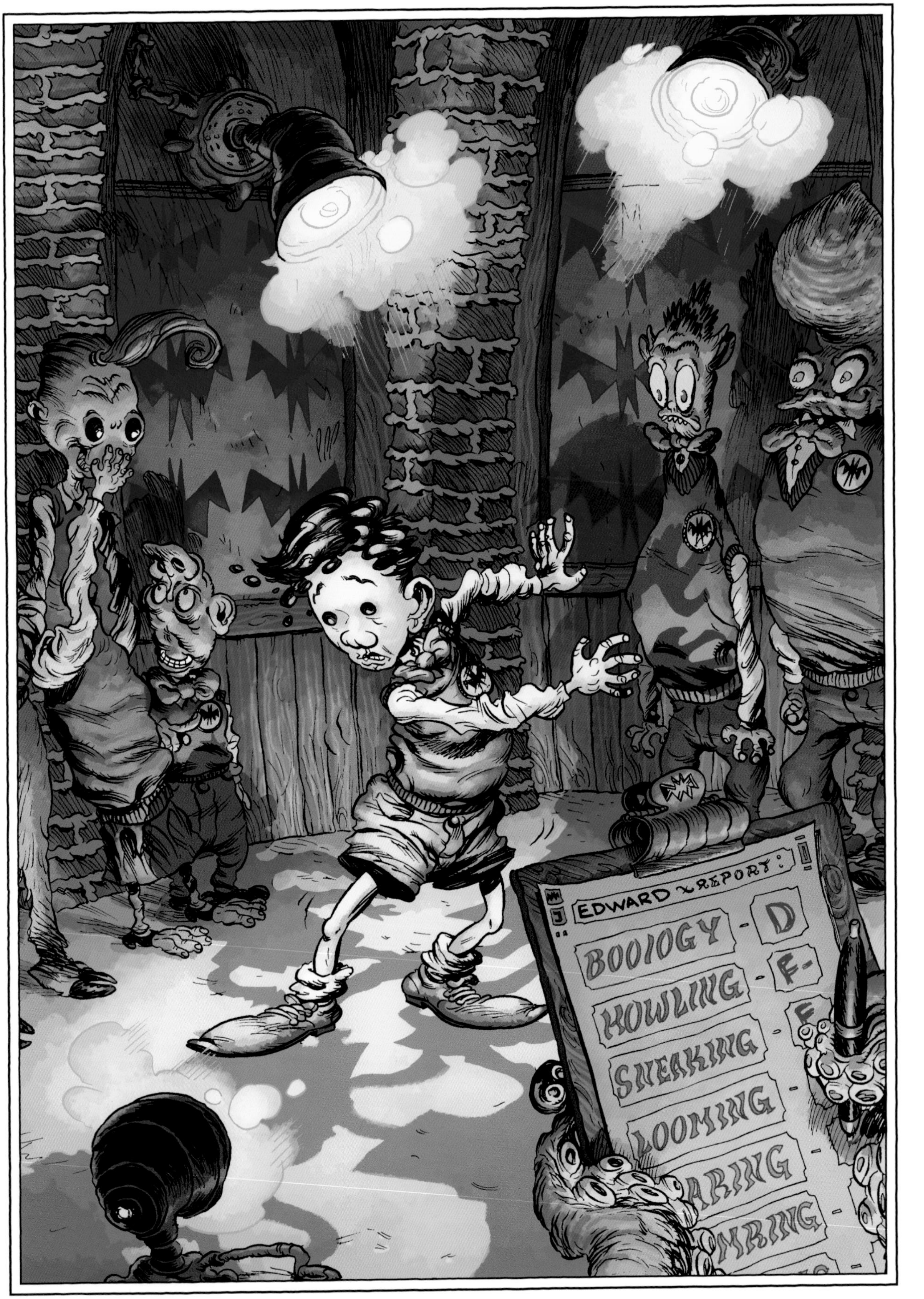

EDWARD REPORT:
BOOIOGY - D
HOWLING - F-
SNEAKING - F
LOOMING -

Then one day the school bully stepped up to claim
that Ed was a blight on his father's good name.
"What kind of a monster . . ." he asked with a sneer,
". . . gets fearful whenever a monster is near?"

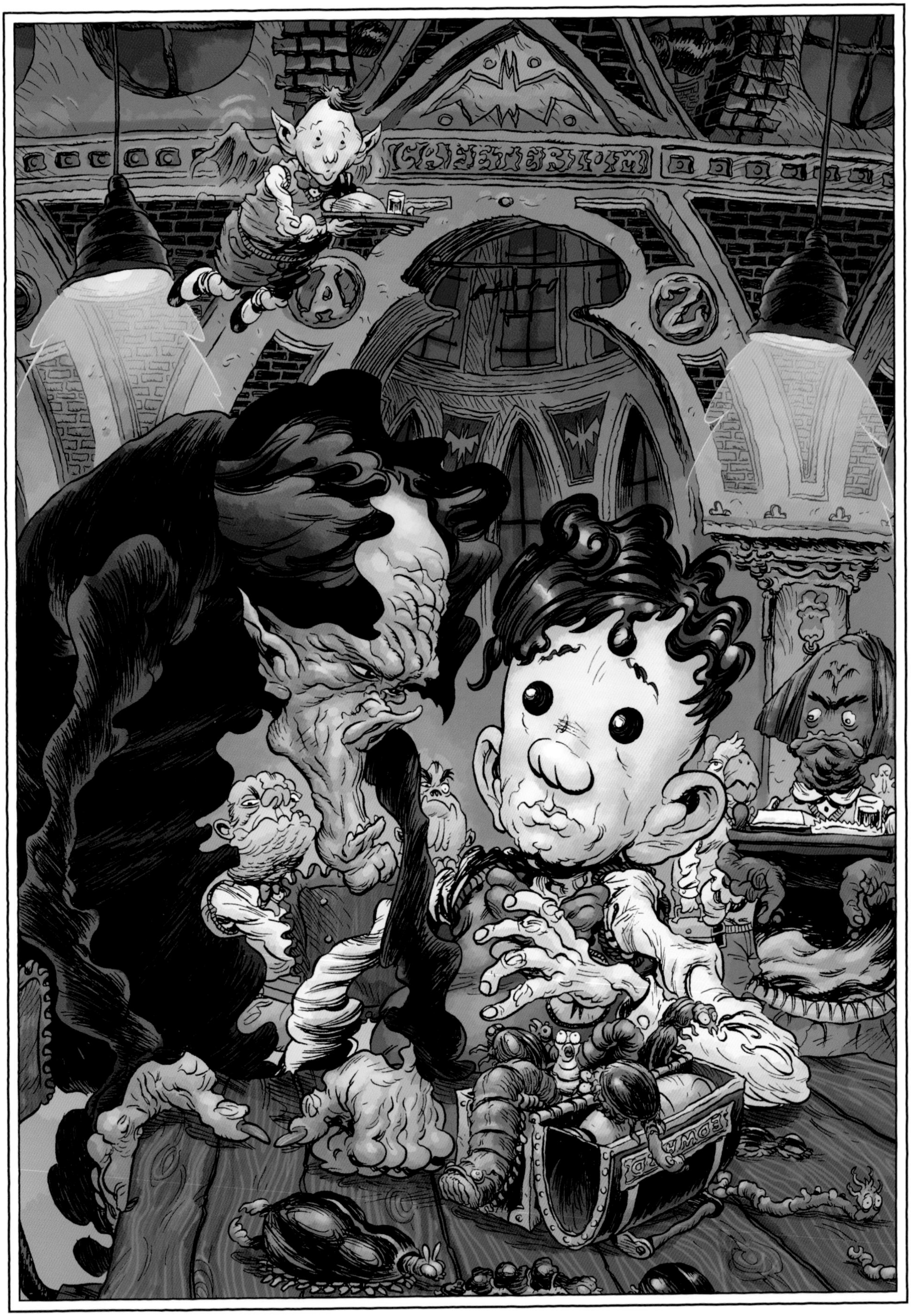

So later that night, Edgar packed up a sack
and ran from his home vowing not to come back.
Afraid of the shame he might bring to his father
and sad he had always been naught but a bother.

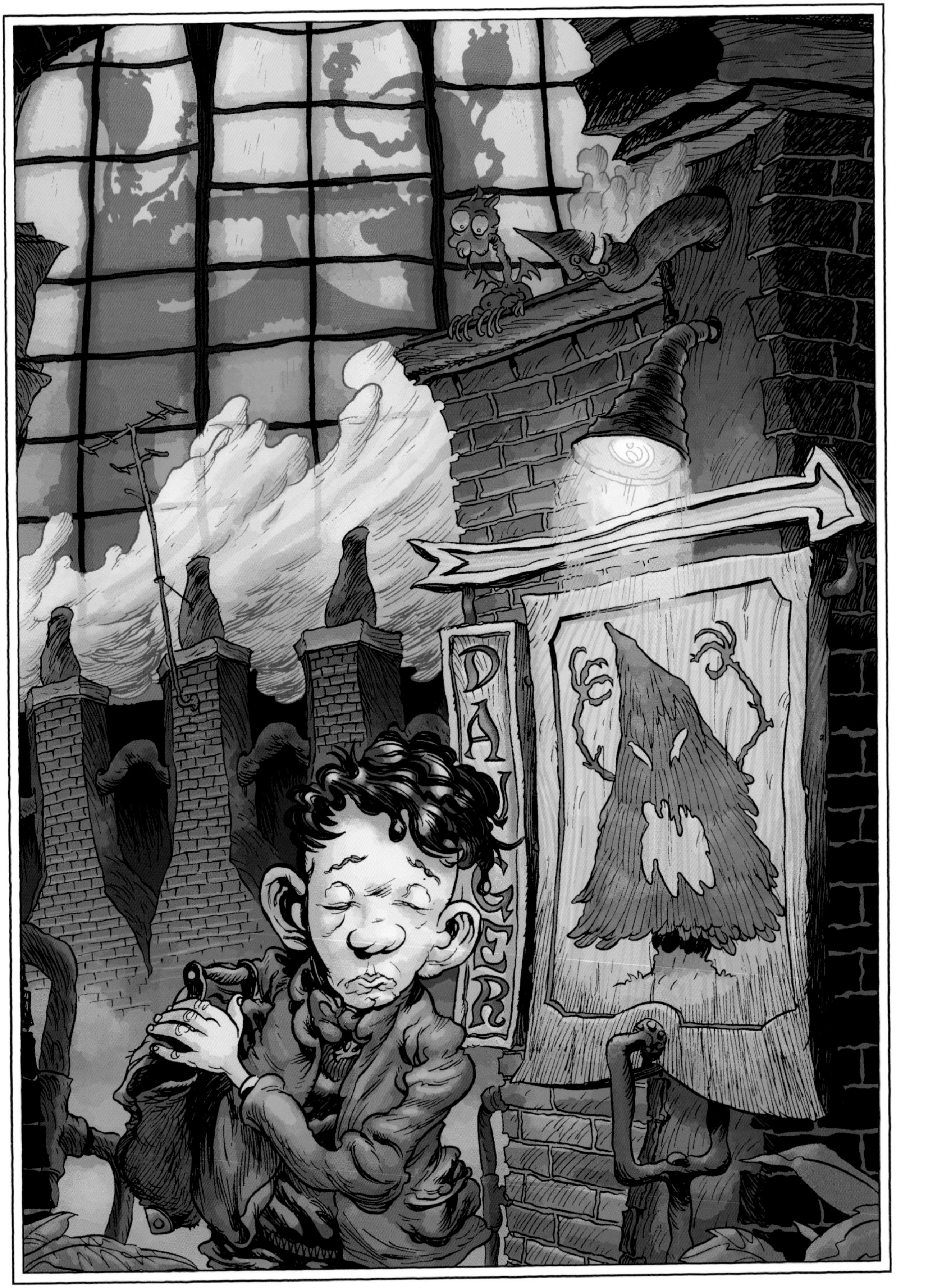

Into the Black Forest, Edgar took flight,
hounded by things that go bump in the night.
Determined to shed off his cowardly ways,
he instead lost his head and got stuck in a maze.

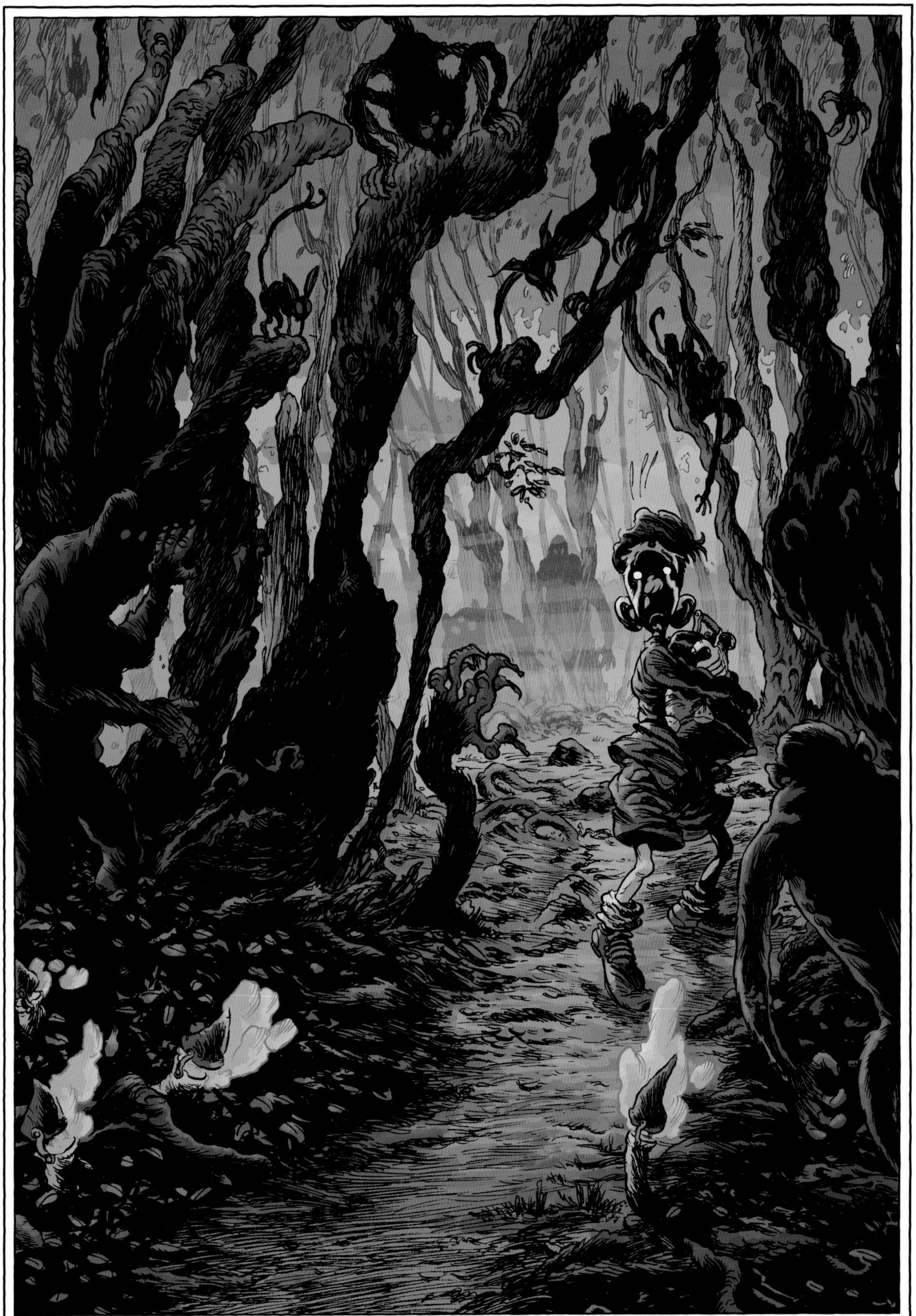

A shadow loomed large over frightened young Ed,
who wished beyond wishing he'd stayed home in bed.
"This is it! It's the end!" he whimpered aloud.
"Now how will I ever make my father proud?"

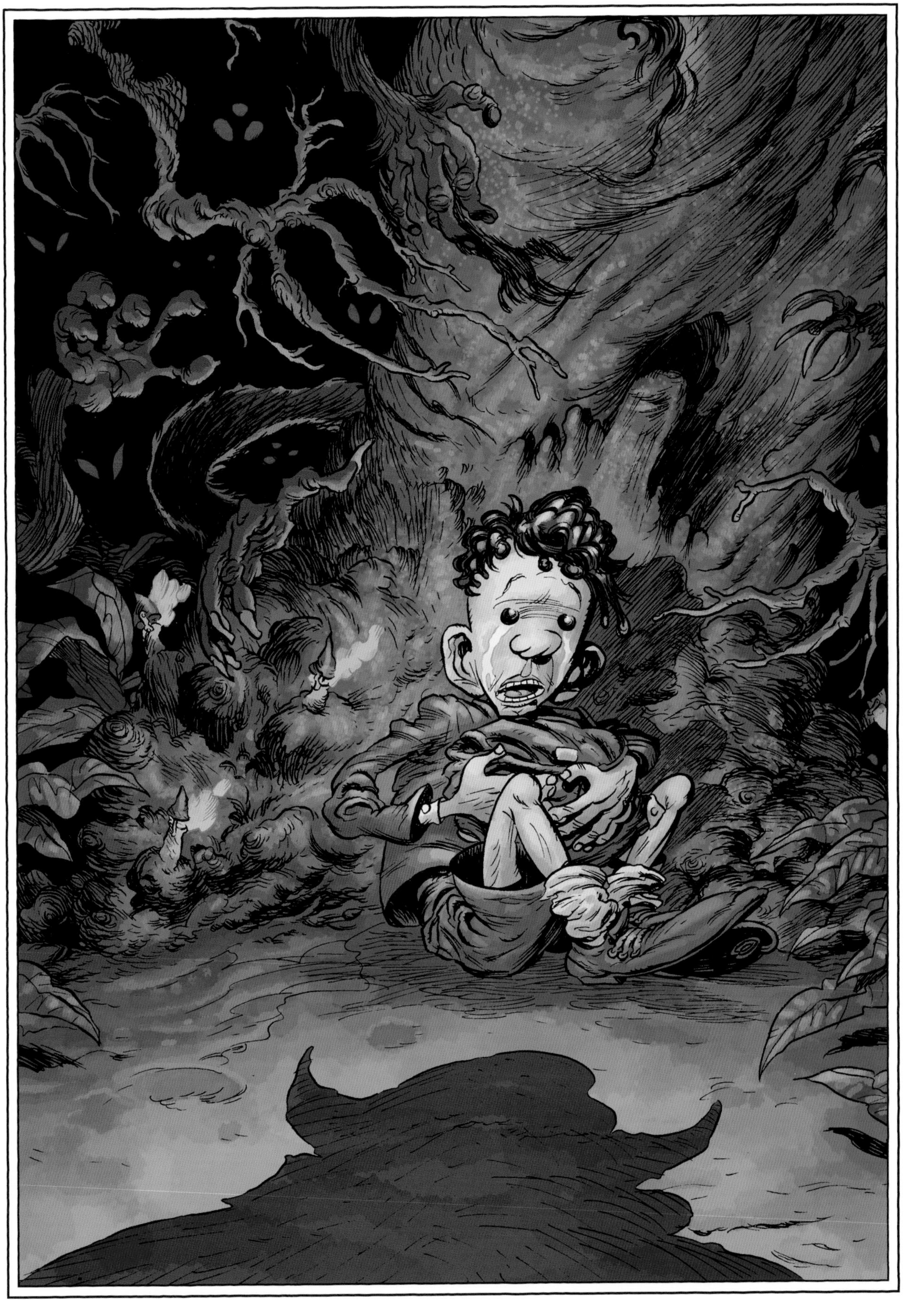

But what happened next came as quite a surprise.

The Boogeyman appeared with tears in his eyes.

He hugged Edgar tightly, then rightly declared,

"I thought I had lost you. I've never been so scared."

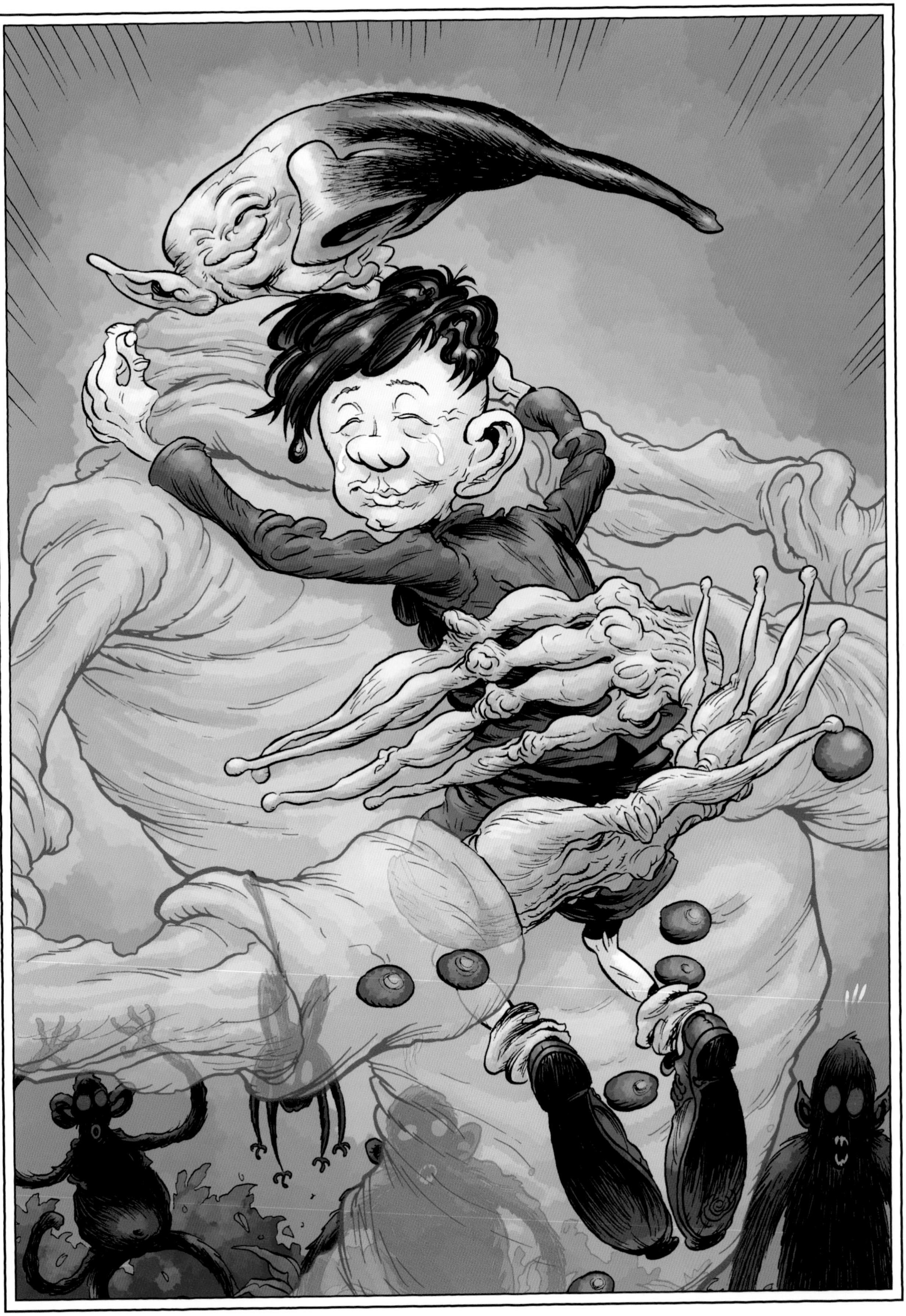

Word quickly spread of what Boogey had said.
He'd been spooked by his own son, the misfit named Ed.
In his struggle to do what just couldn't be done,
a boy found his father, and a father—his son.

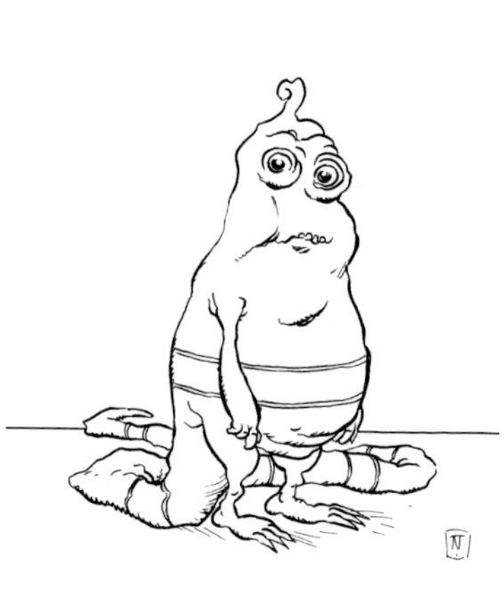

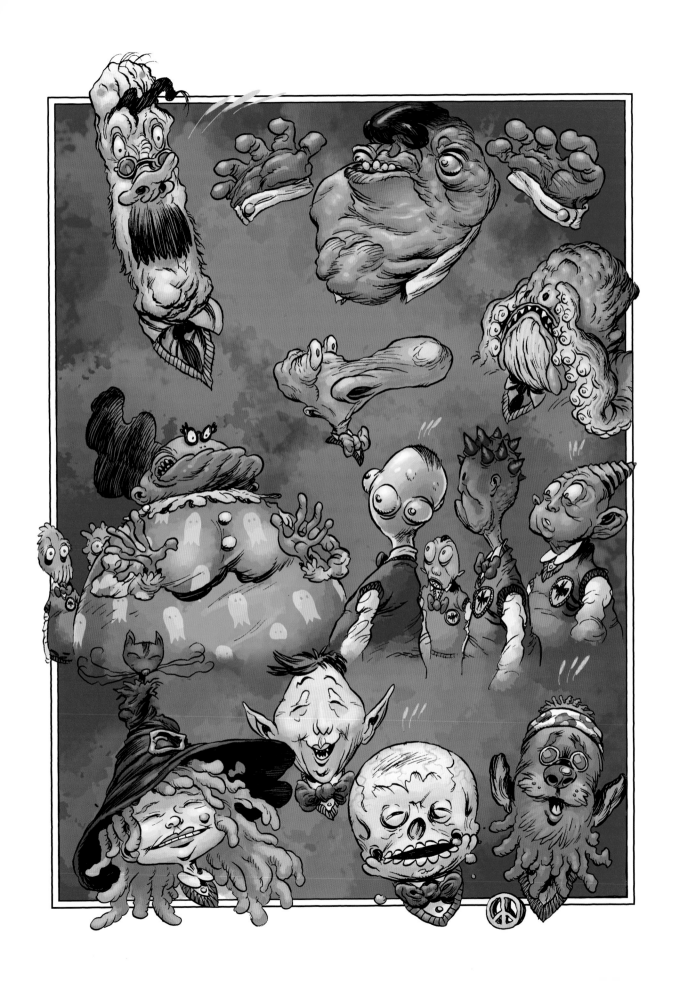

So come graduation, with no hesitation
Ed passed, head of class, and to much jubilation.
The crowd looked on proudly, all save for Lenore,
who knew secretly there's more of this story in store . . .

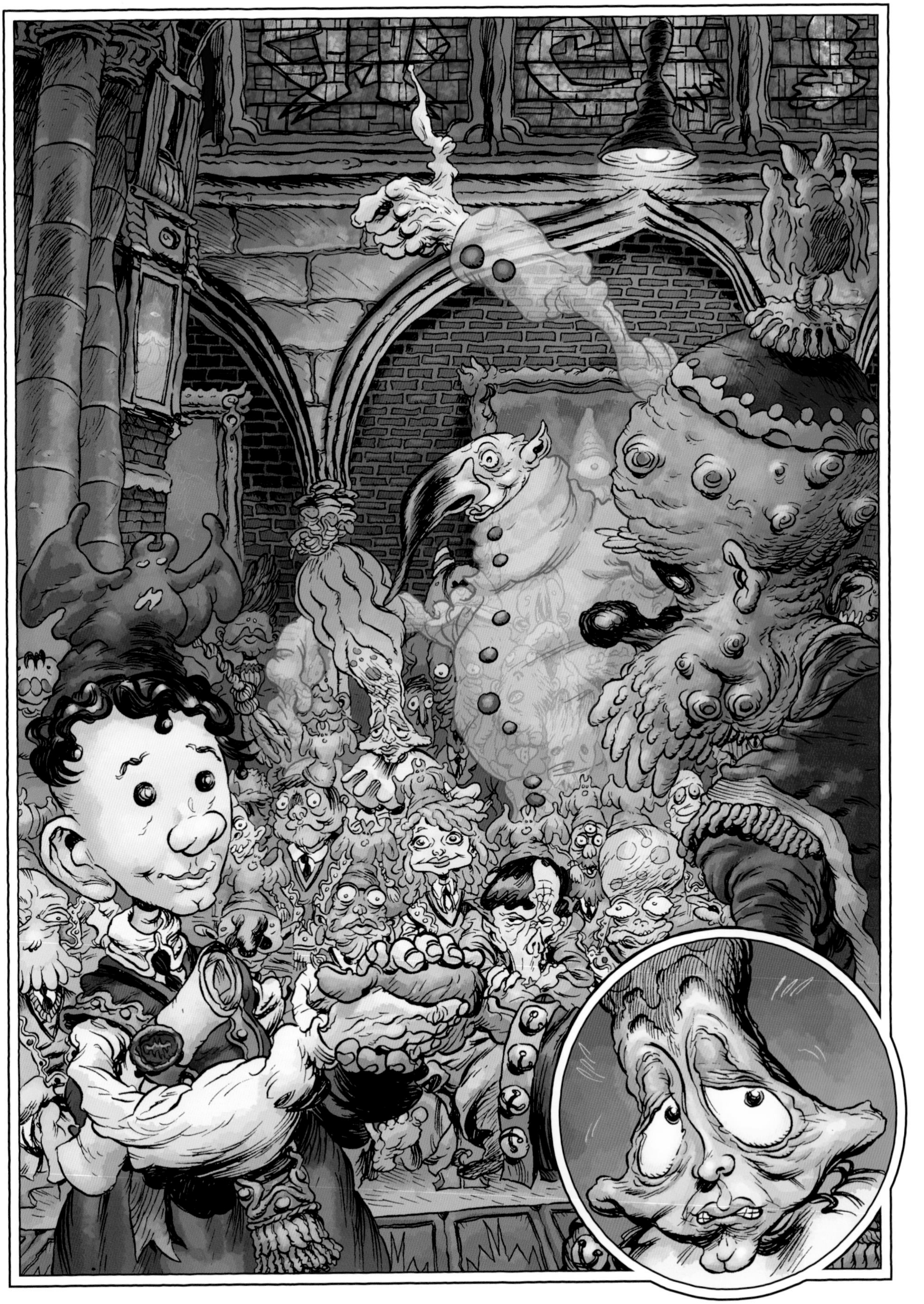

For somewhere out there, yet to be seen
is Boogey's real daughter, lucky number thirteen,
a strange little girl who doesn't try to be scary
but is nonetheless . . .

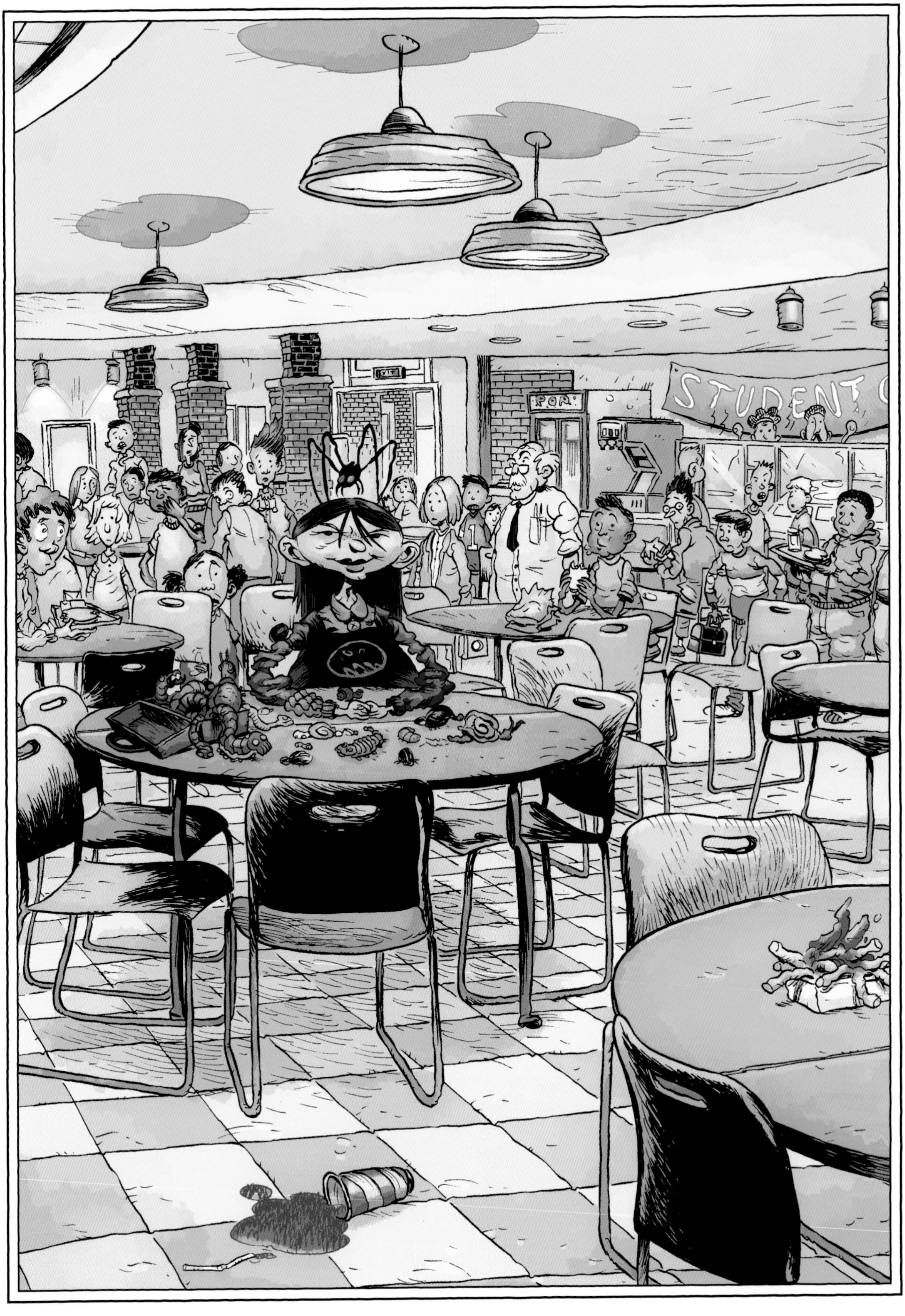
STUDENT
POP

. . . and her name is *Mary*.

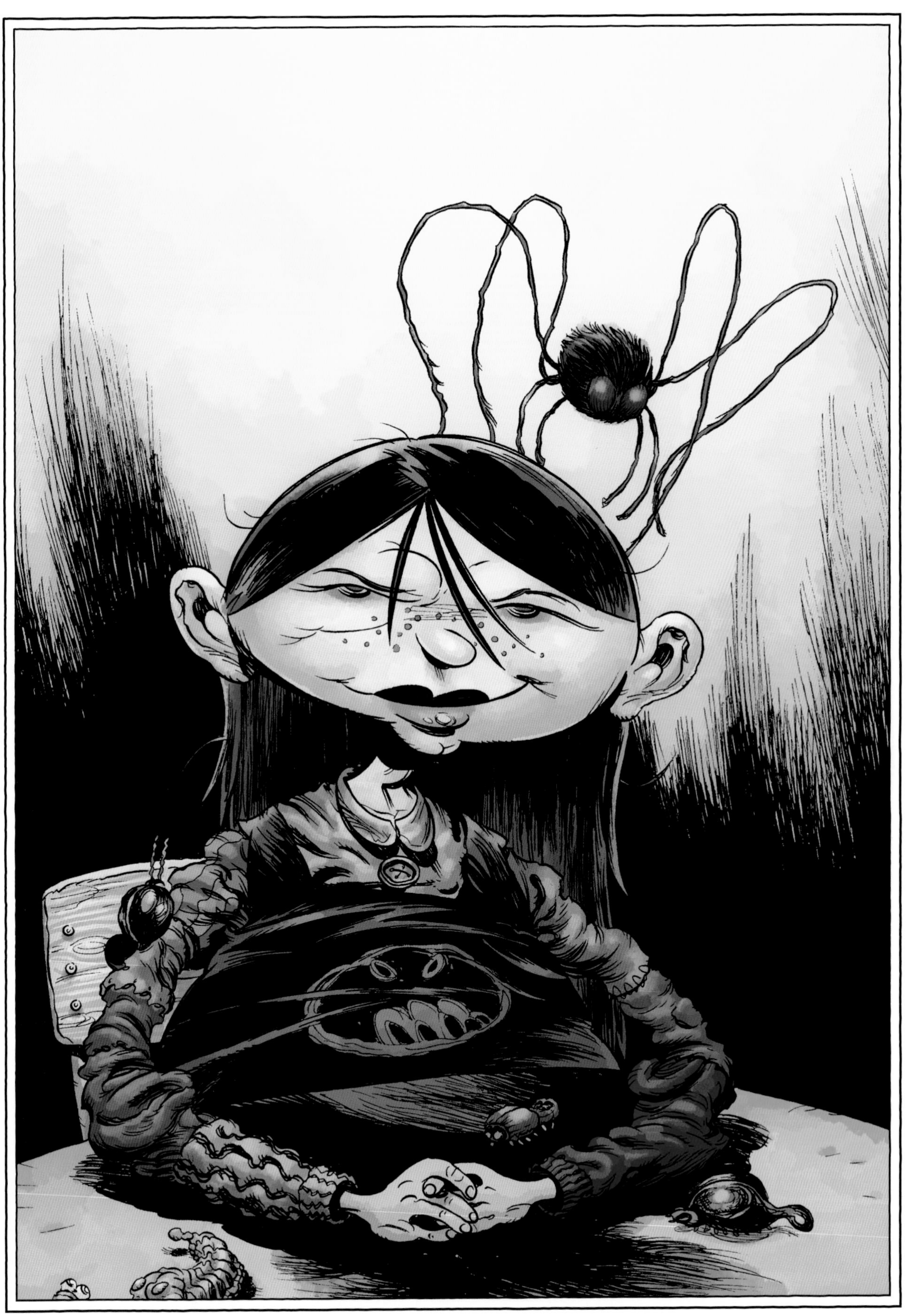

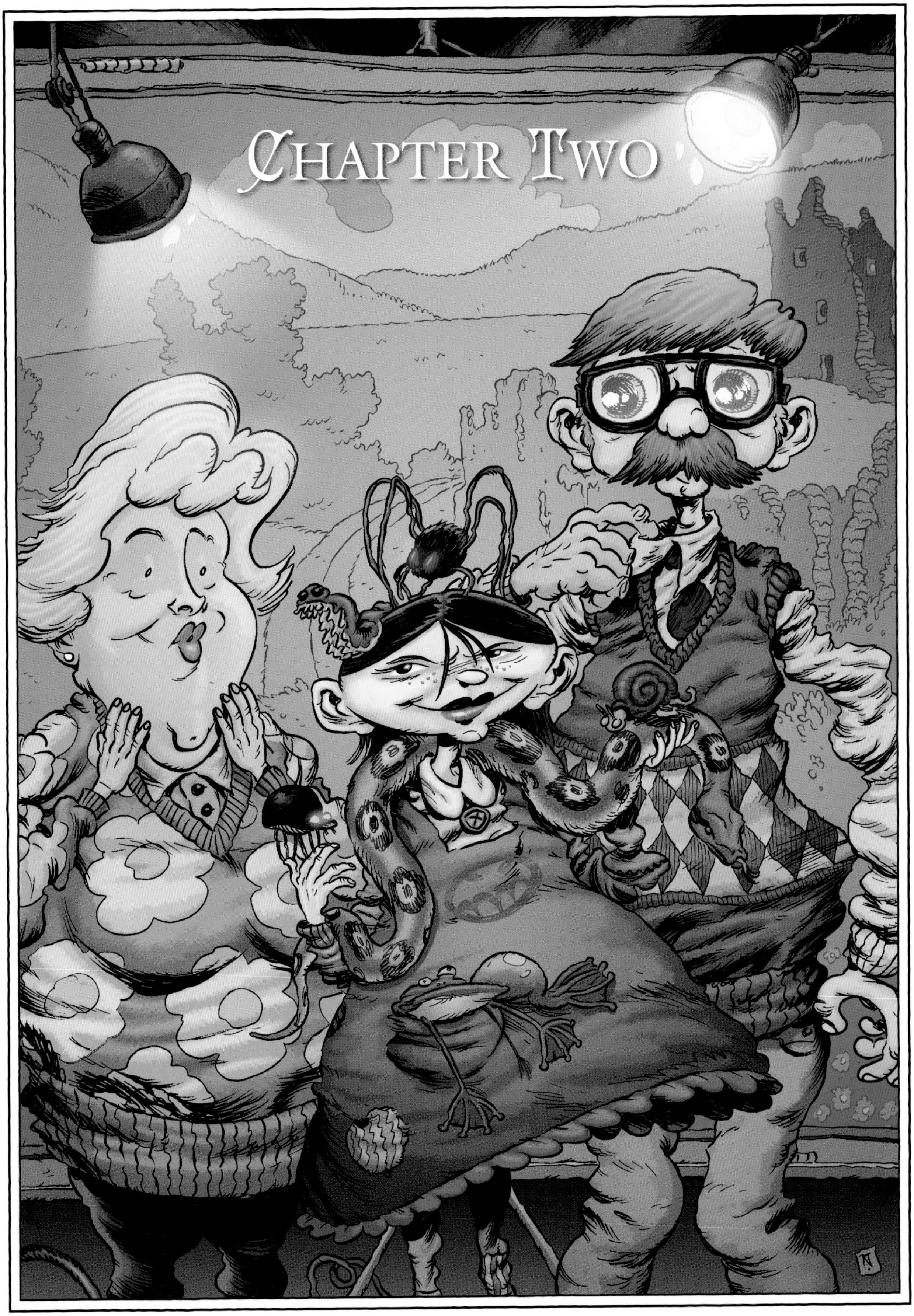
CHAPTER TWO

There once was a girl not much like you or me
who was dropped off one night around thirteen past three.
They found her outside in this strange bassinet
with a handwritten note that began, "I regret . . .

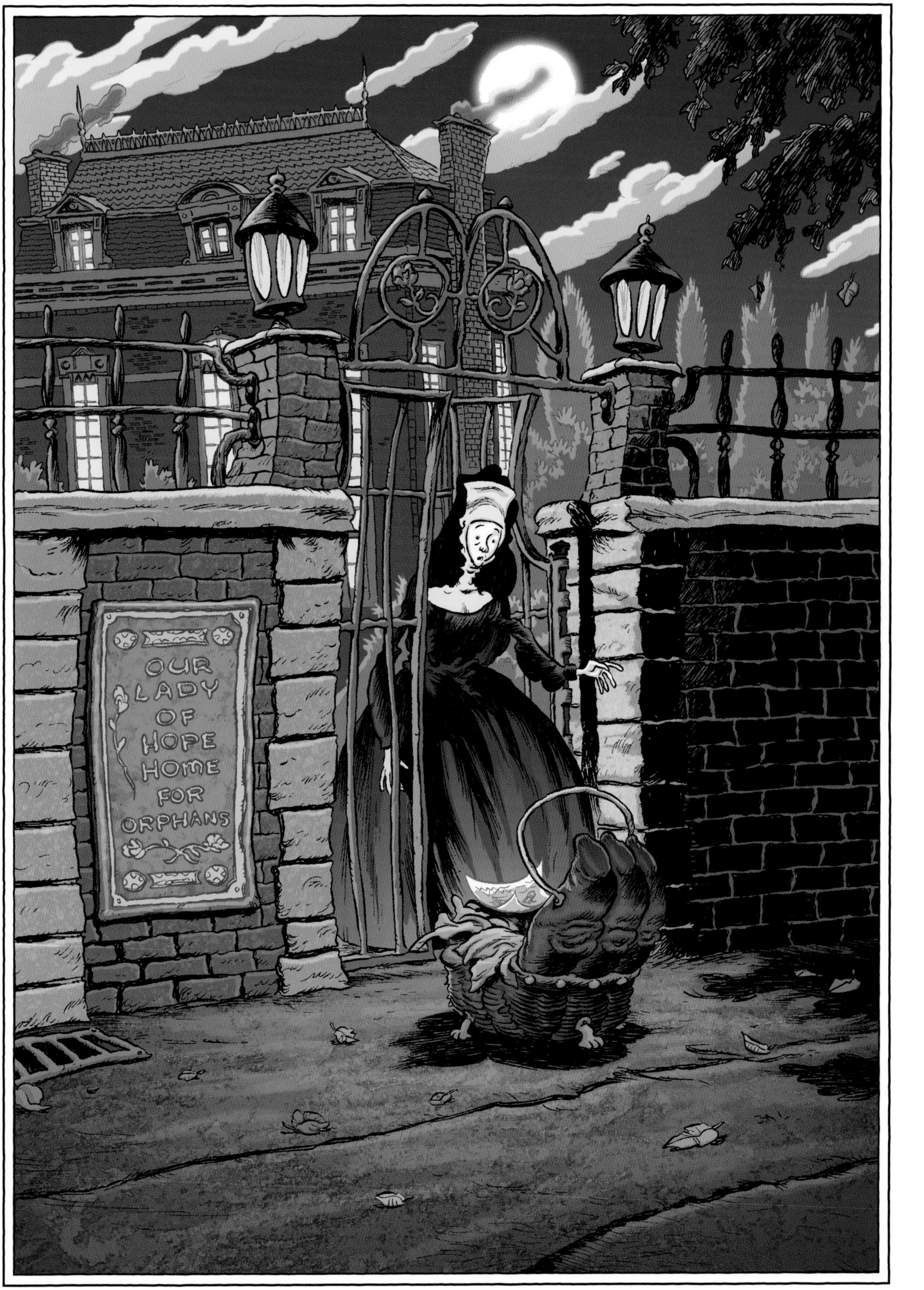
OUR LADY OF HOPE HOME FOR ORPHANS

I am forced to give up this most wonderful girl
who no doubt you can tell is not from your world.
She was born in a place not at all like your own,
but please raise her with love and then find her a home."

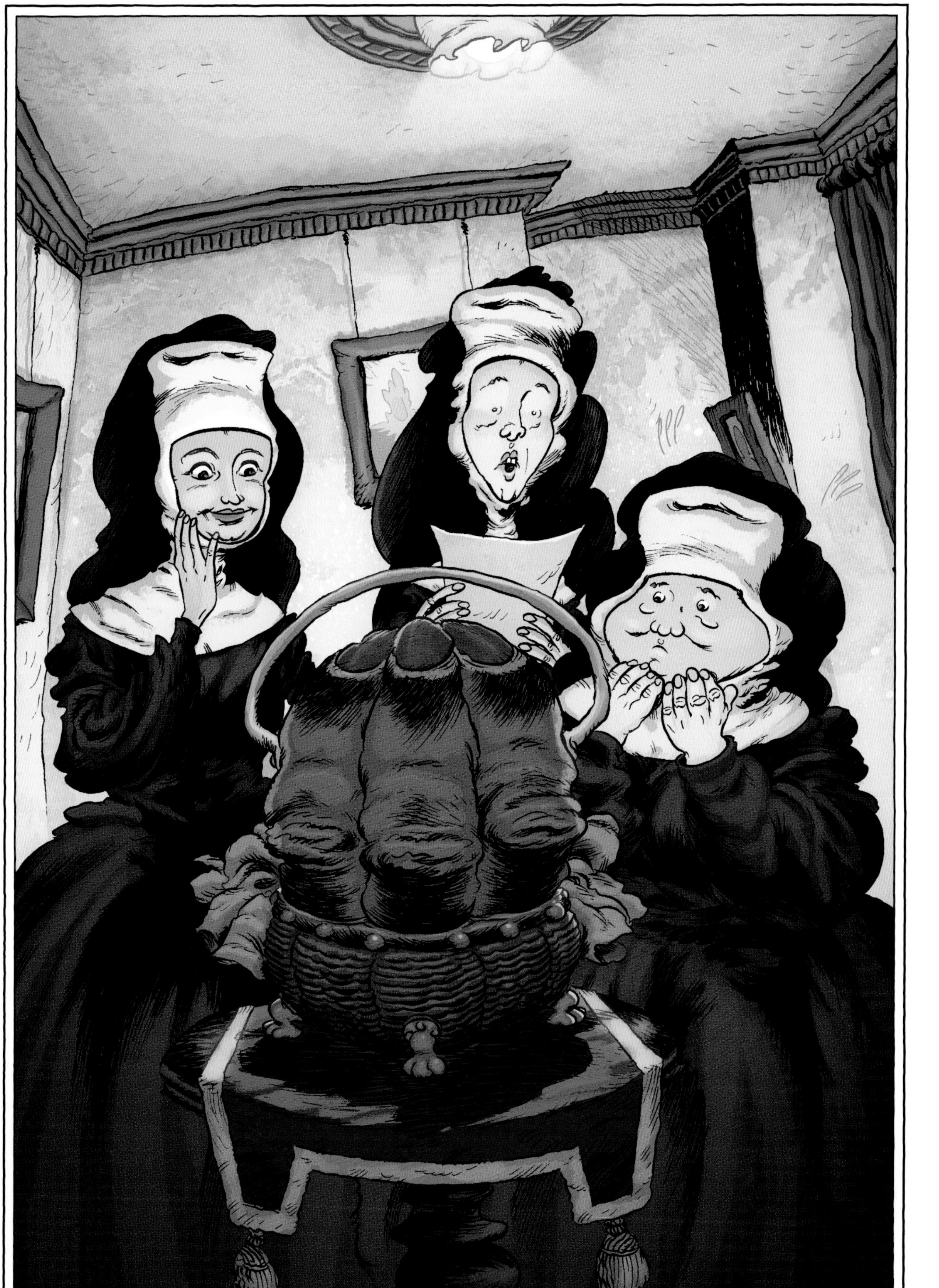

The nuns stared wide-eyed, not quite sure what to do.

When it comes to good homes, there are always too few.

The last thing they needed was one orphan more,

yet here was this dear who'd been left at their door.

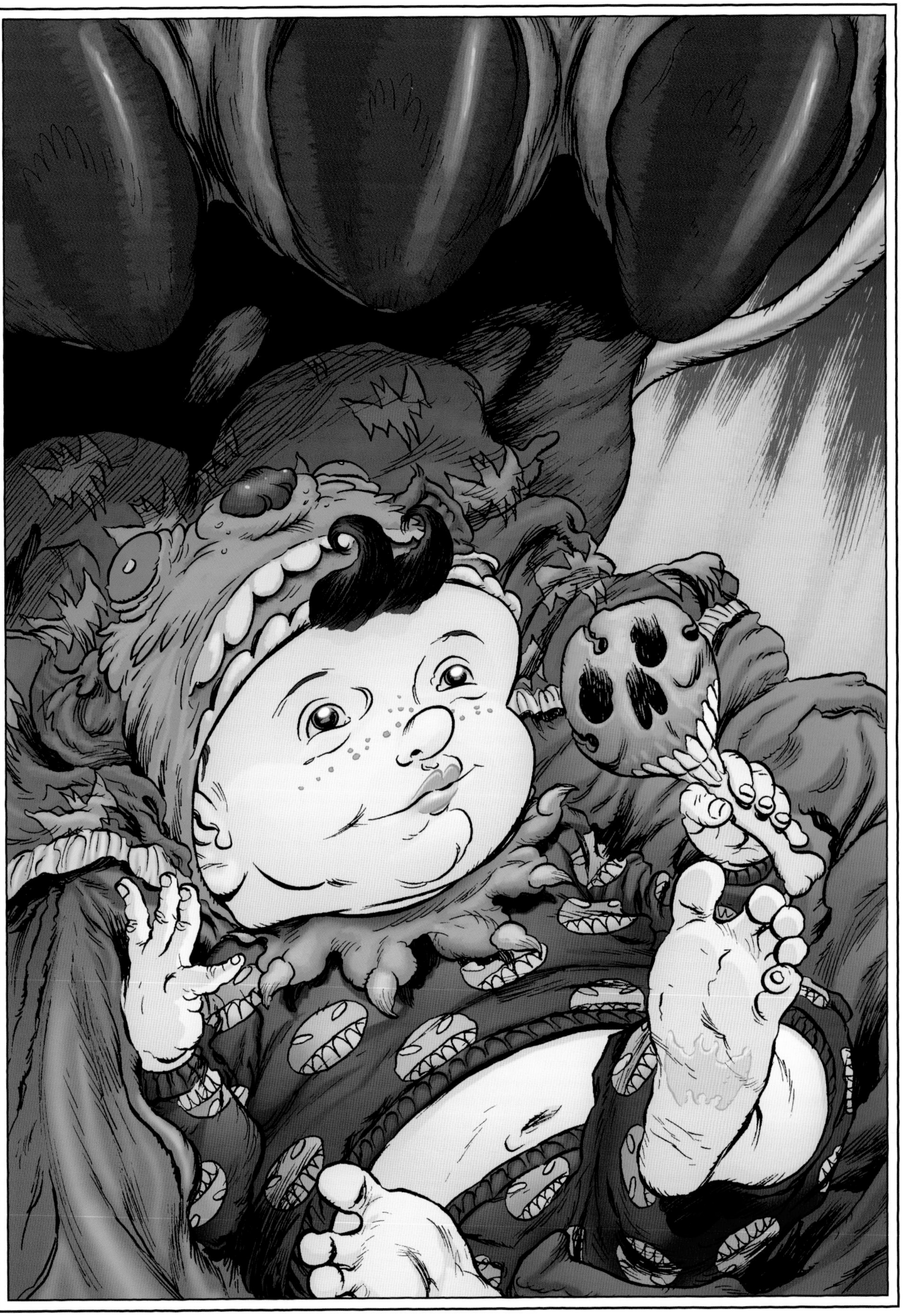

They called the girl Mary, and raised her up right.
They rocked her and fed her, read stories at night.
When Mary would cry, they would sing her a song,
but it didn't take long to tell Mary was . . . wrong.

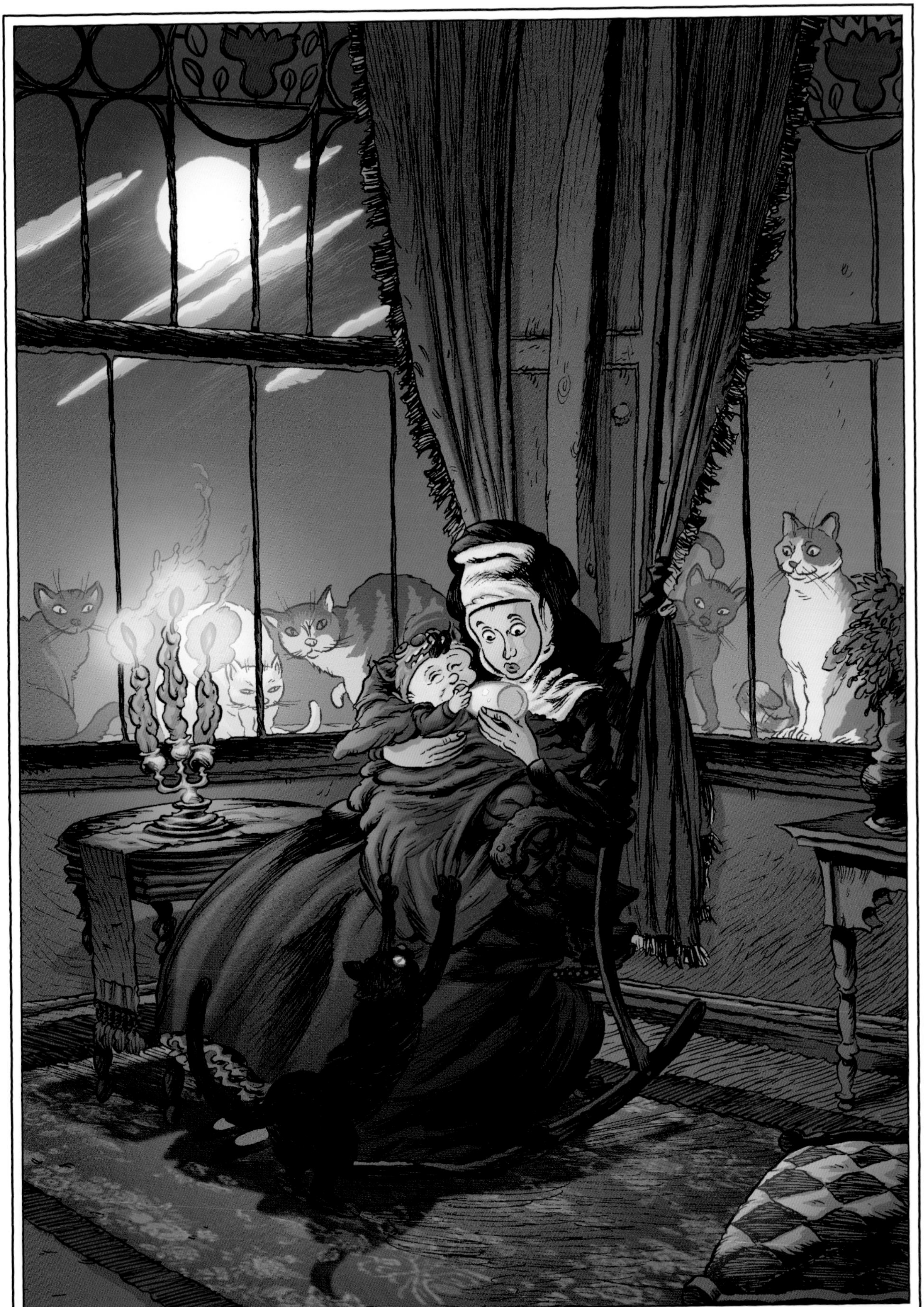

Little Mary wasn't like other children her age.
Exactly how different, they just couldn't gauge,
but her dolls had no heads, she dressed all in black,
and when folks would adopt her, she'd always come back.

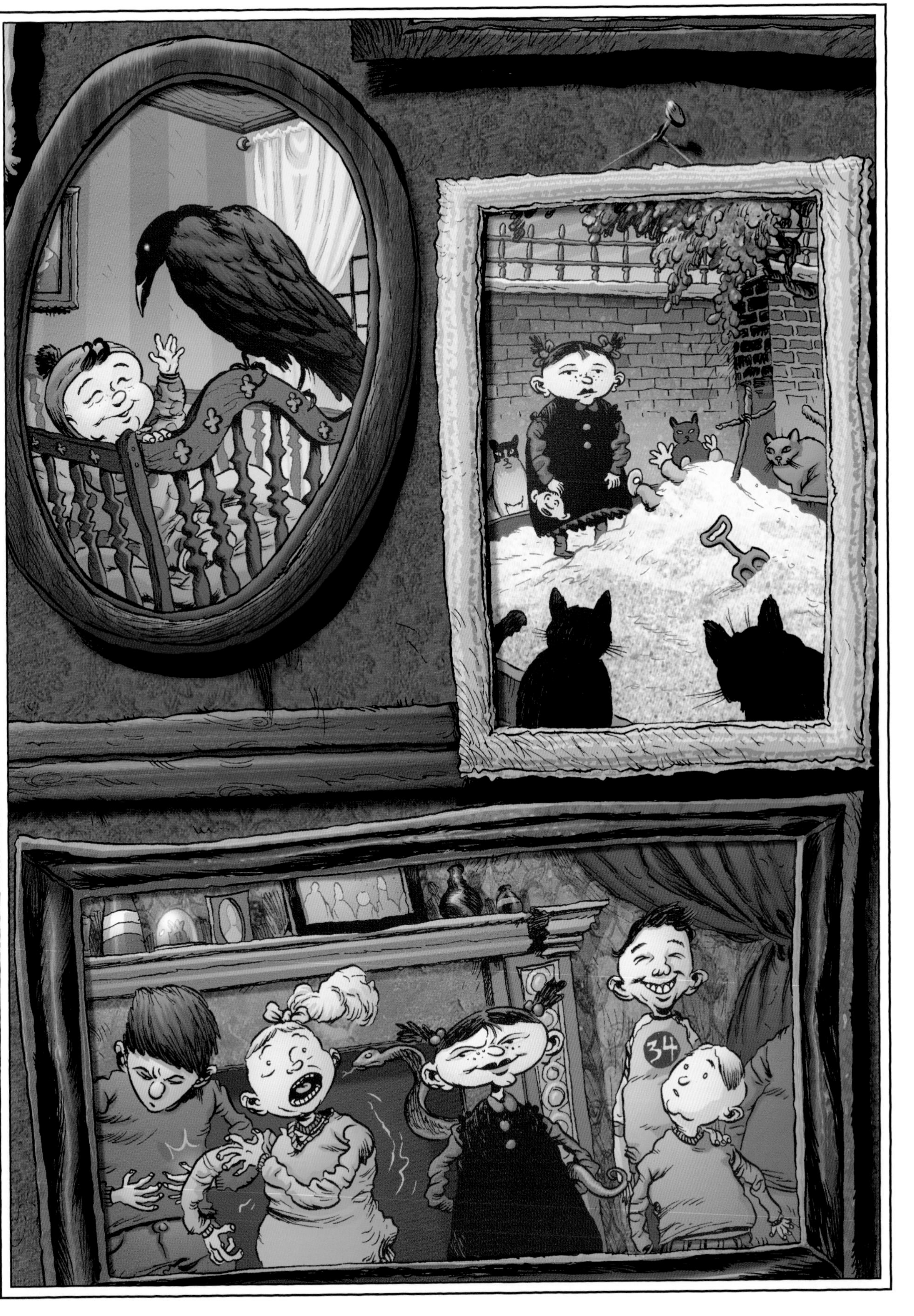
34

It's said that young girls are all sugar and spice,
that they're made from ingredients both proper and nice.
But as for our Mary, this just isn't true.
She's all slimy snakes, rats and bats, grimy goo.

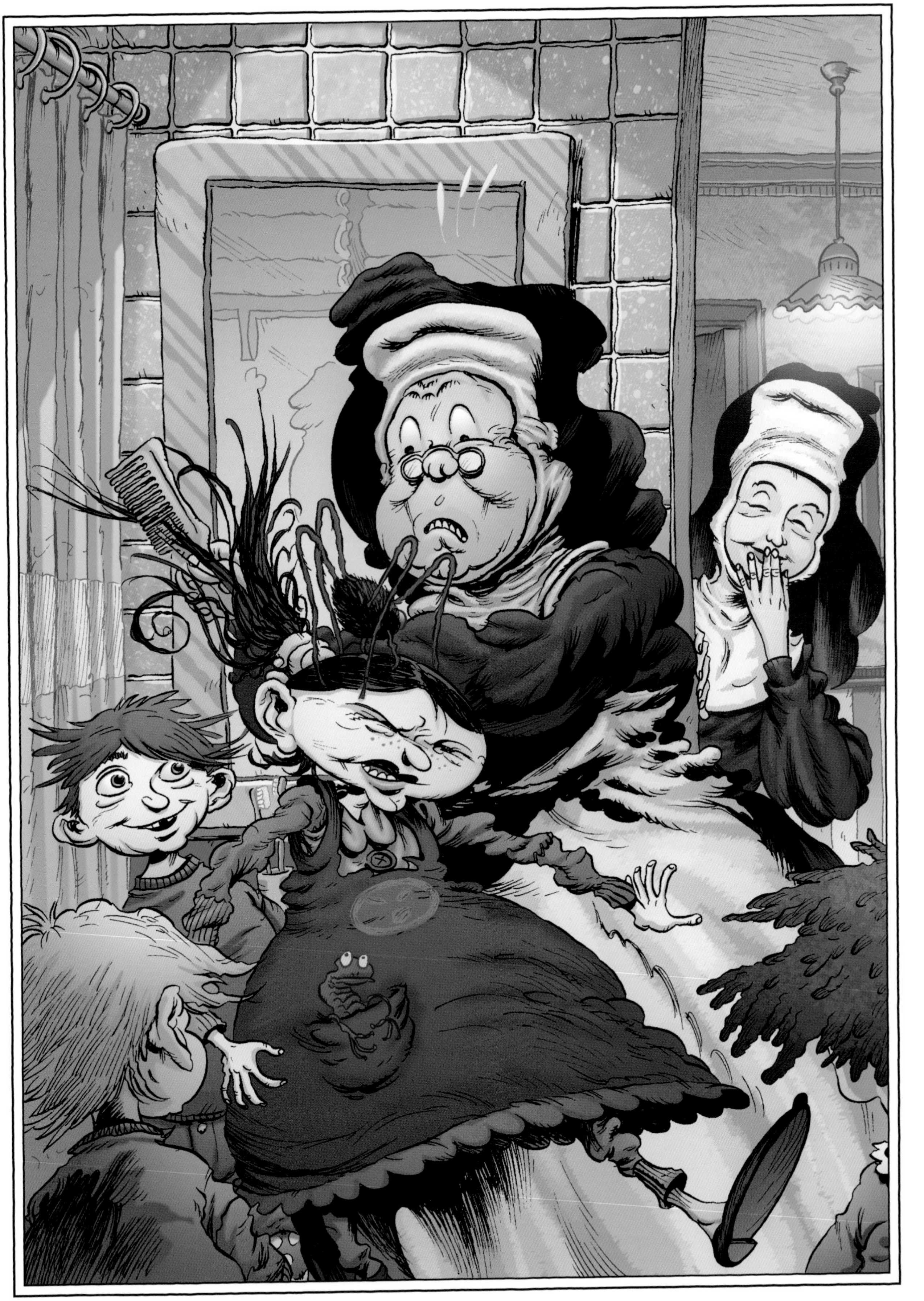

In Mary's case, when it comes to adoption
she's not like the rest, so there's only one option.
Cross fingers and toes and try to arrange
for a pair who might share in her taste for the strange.

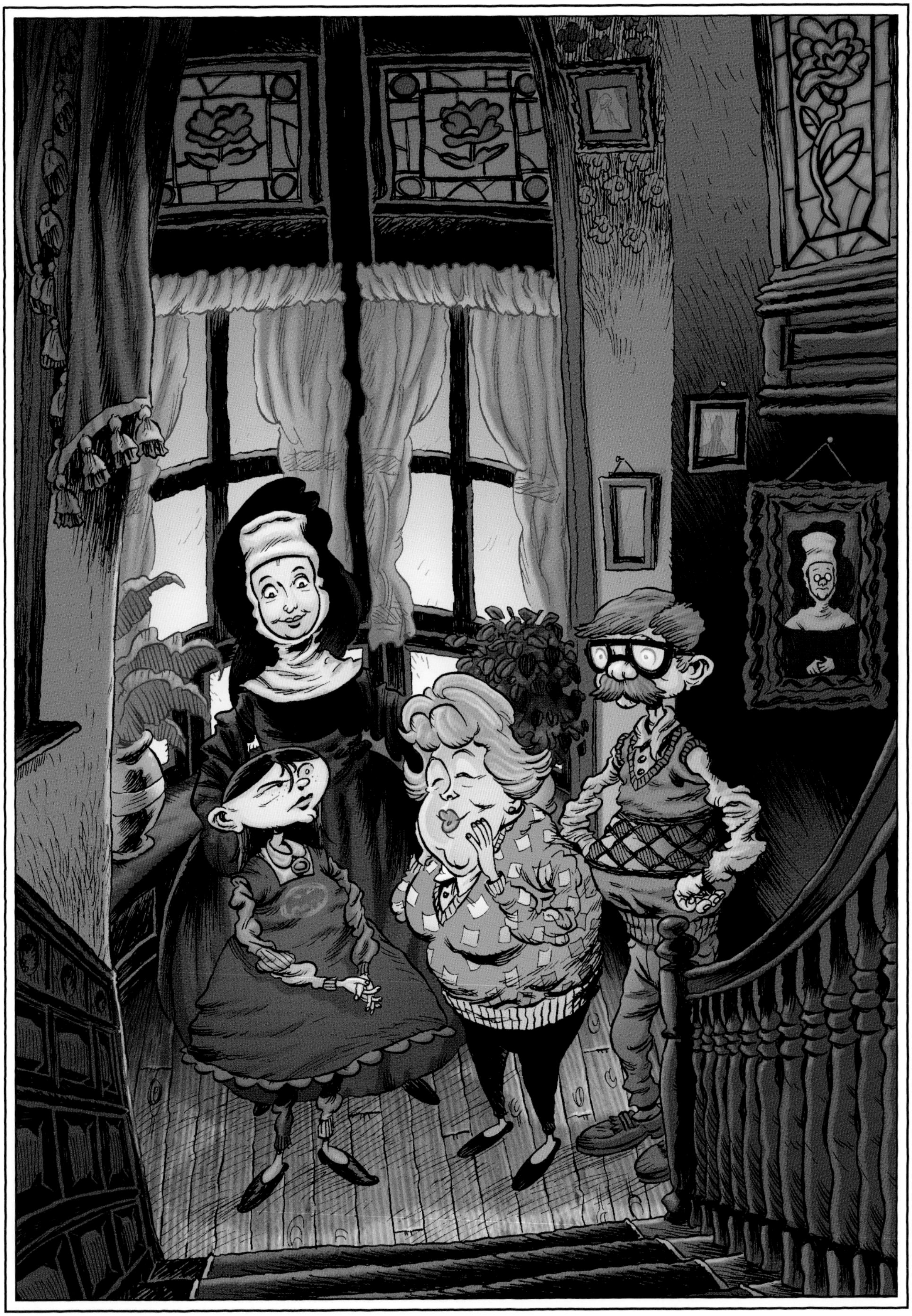

And thanks to the stars, it happened one day—a nice couple arrived to take Mary away to a quaint little home on a quiet little street, to be raised by new parents, Martha and Pete.

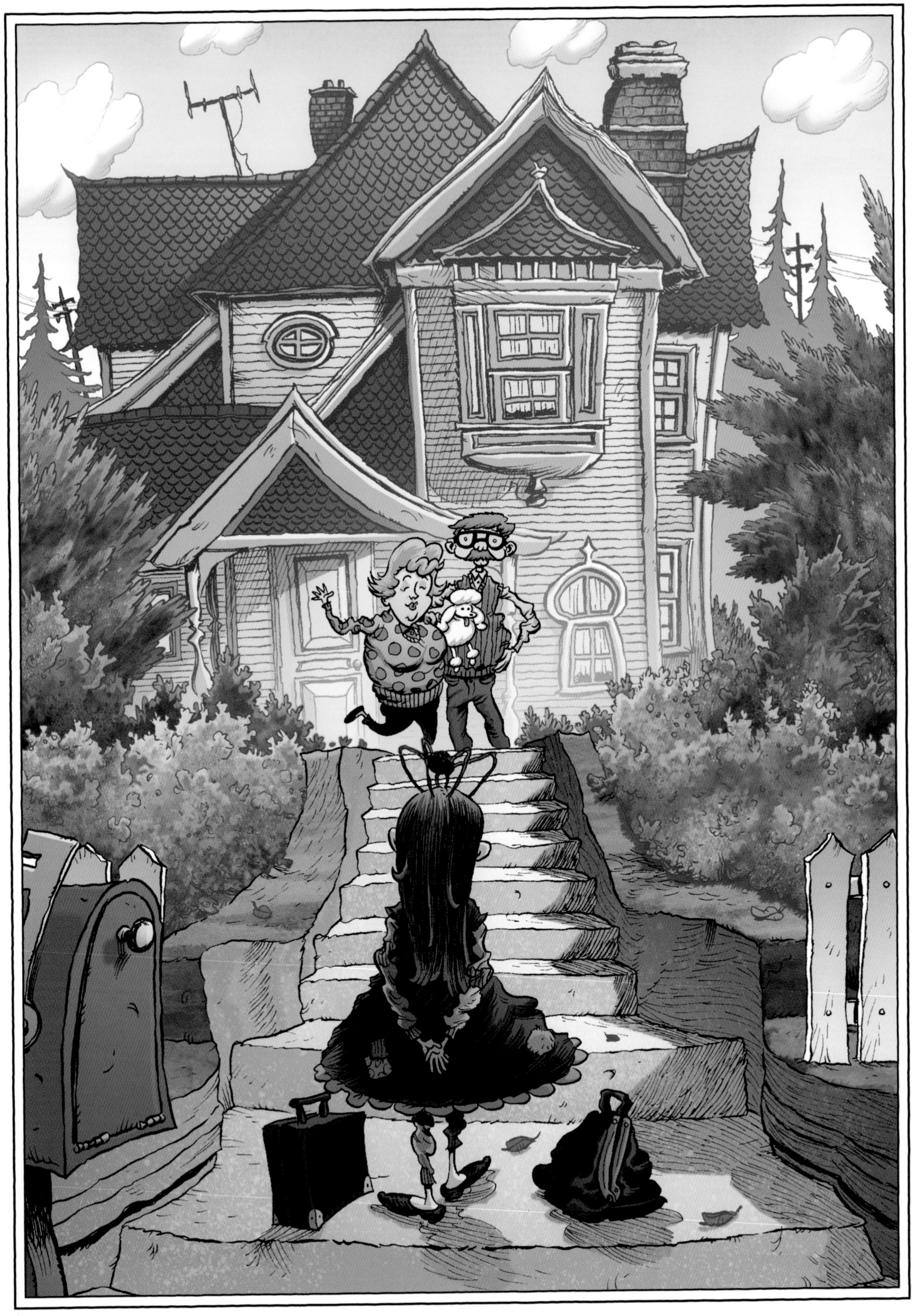

Alone in her room, Mary made a solemn vow:
this time she'd be normal if she could figure out how.
With all of her might she would fight to fit in,
all despite that she didn't know where to begin.

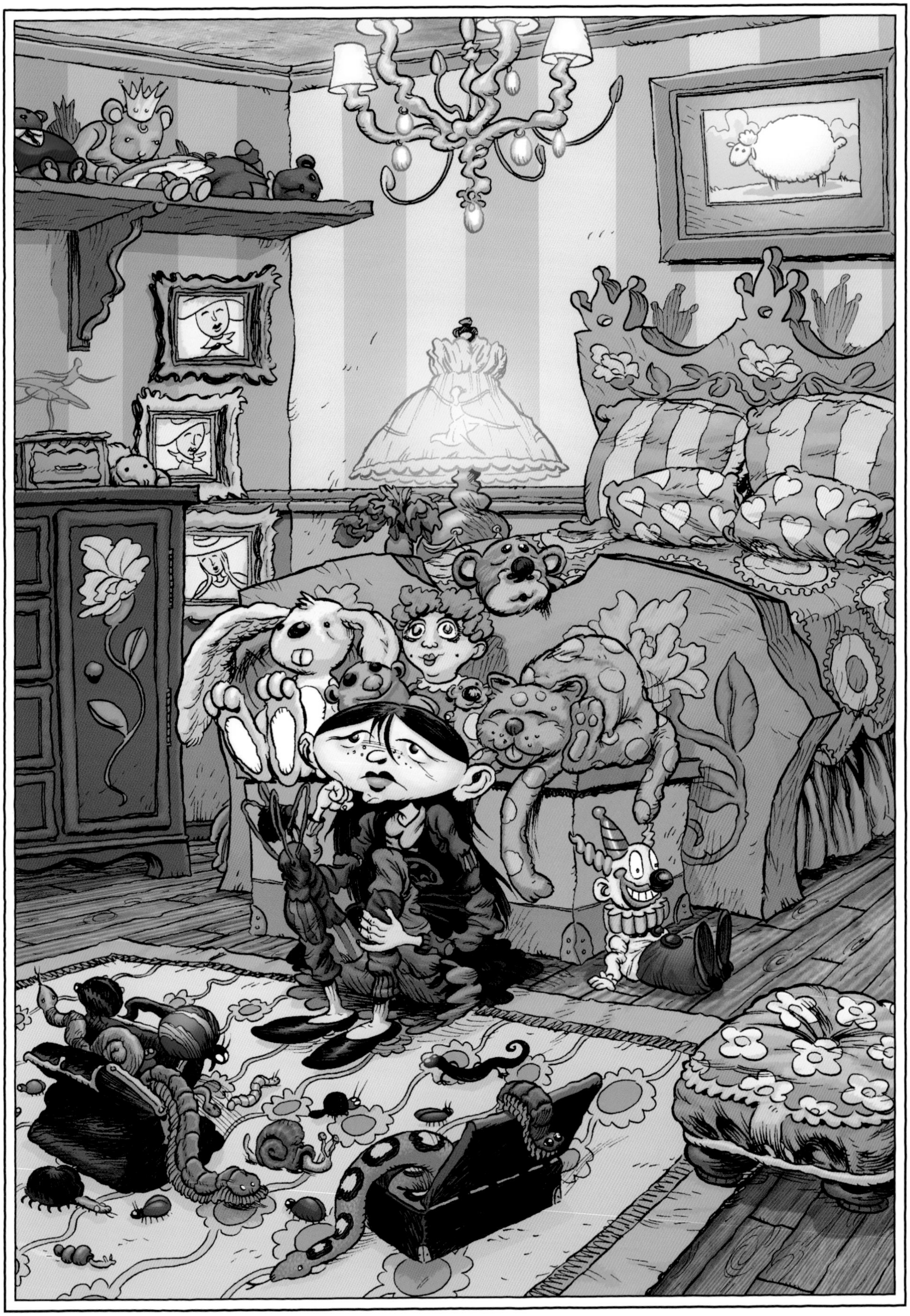

But fitting in wasn't what Mary did well.
She was so very scary, the others could tell
by the way that she walked and she talked and she dressed
that Mary was different, just not like the rest.

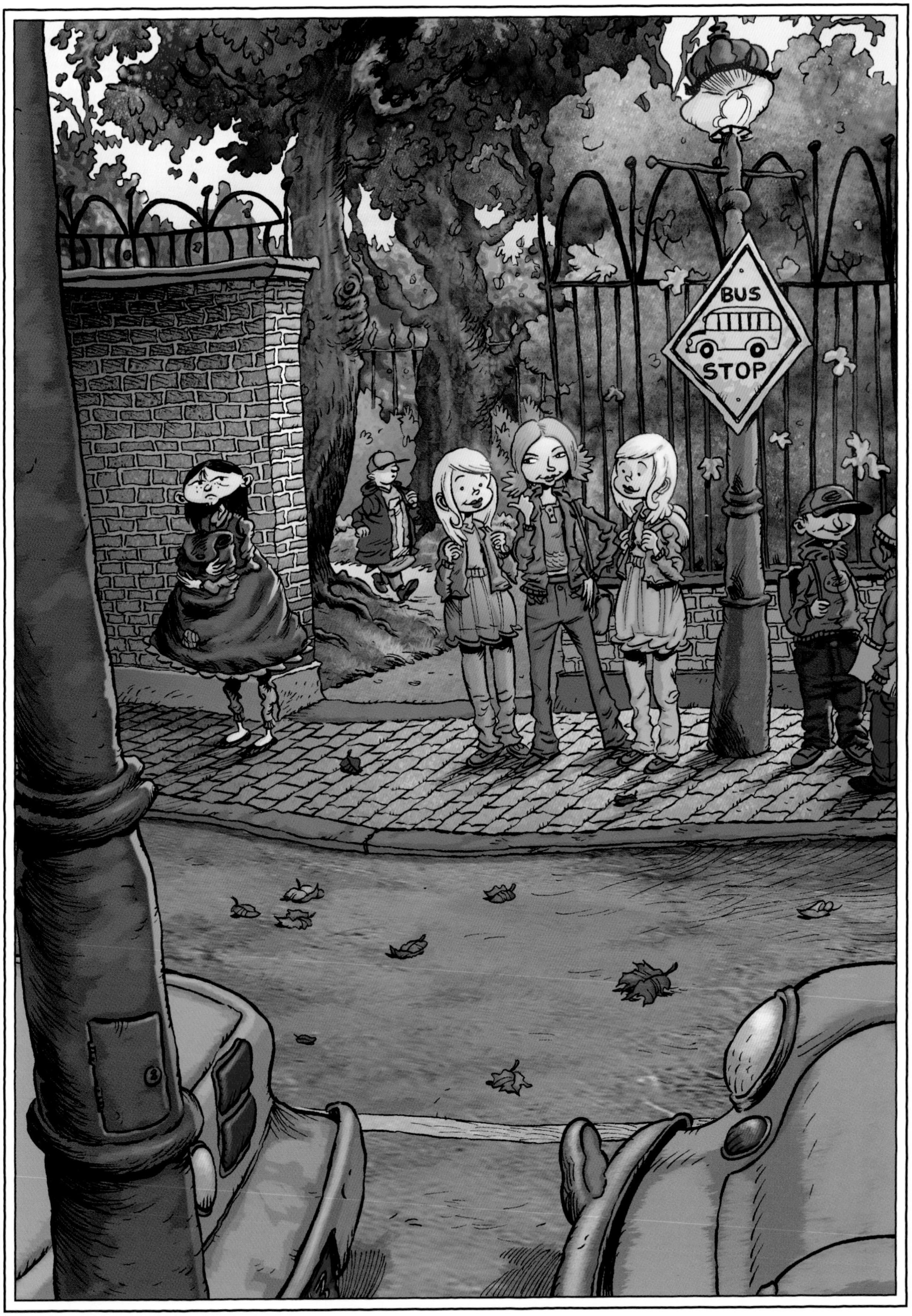
BUS
STOP

The girls in her class would harass and poke fun.
"You're weird, Mary Scary," they would say, every one.
"And since you're the weirdest girl we've ever seen,
we've decided to be you come this Halloween."

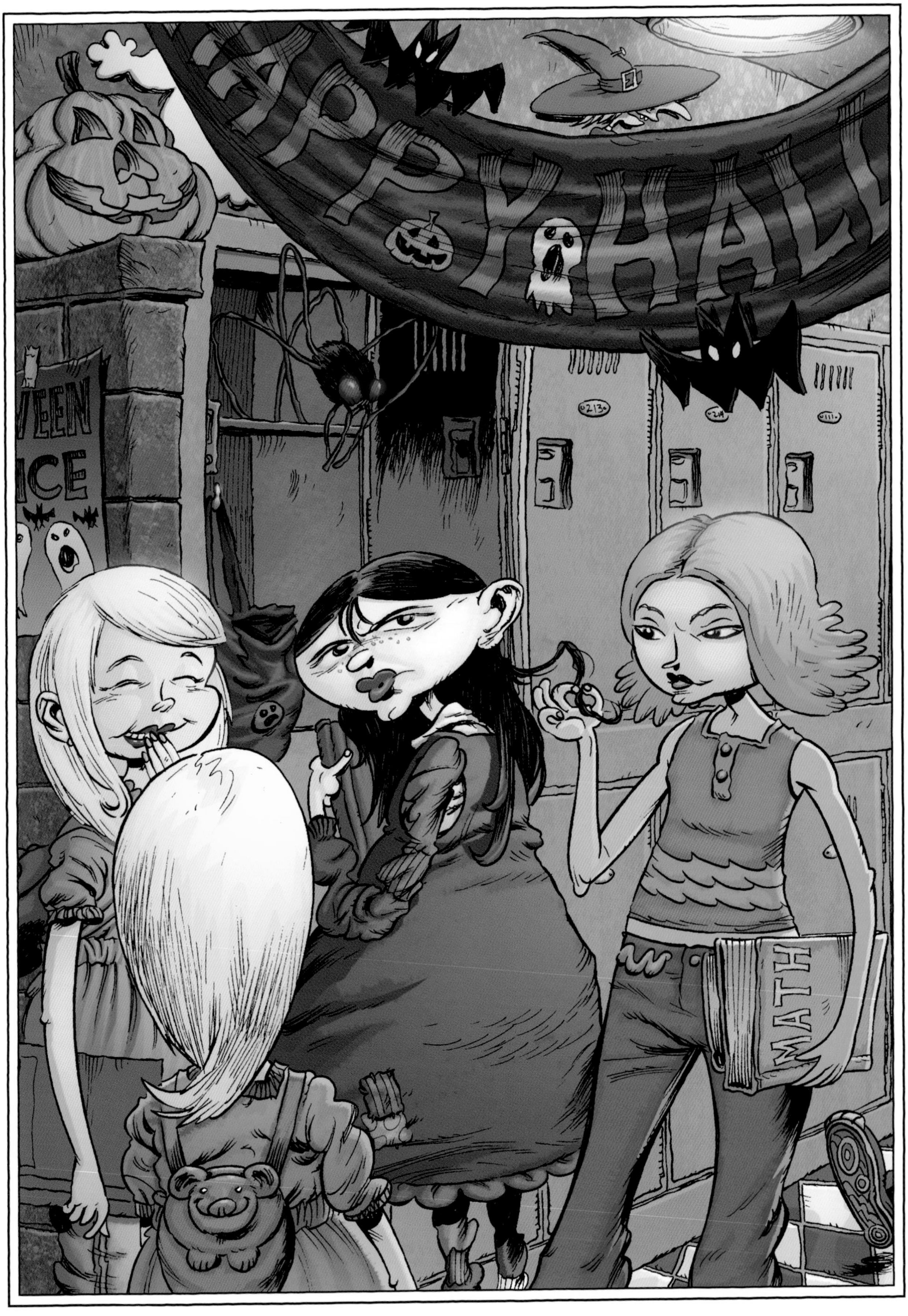
MATH

They showed her their costumes, black dresses and shoes,
fake spiders and snakes, rubber bugs and green ooze.
The other kids laughed when they spied this display.
Mary just sighed and then went on her way.

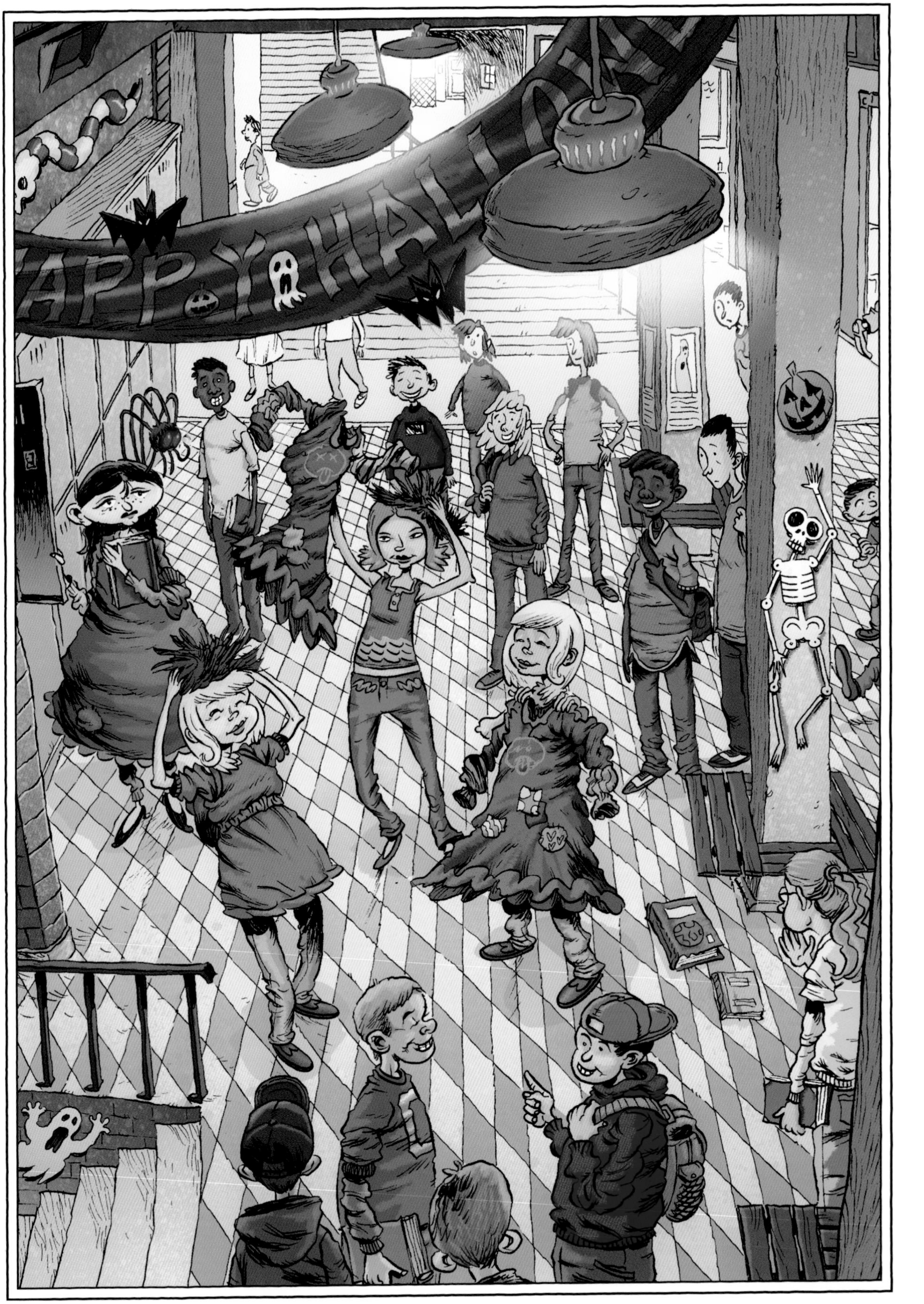

After school she ran home feeling lost and alone,
the worst kind of feeling that she'd ever known.
Halloween was supposed to be fun and delightful,
but for poor Mary Scary, it was just simply frightful.

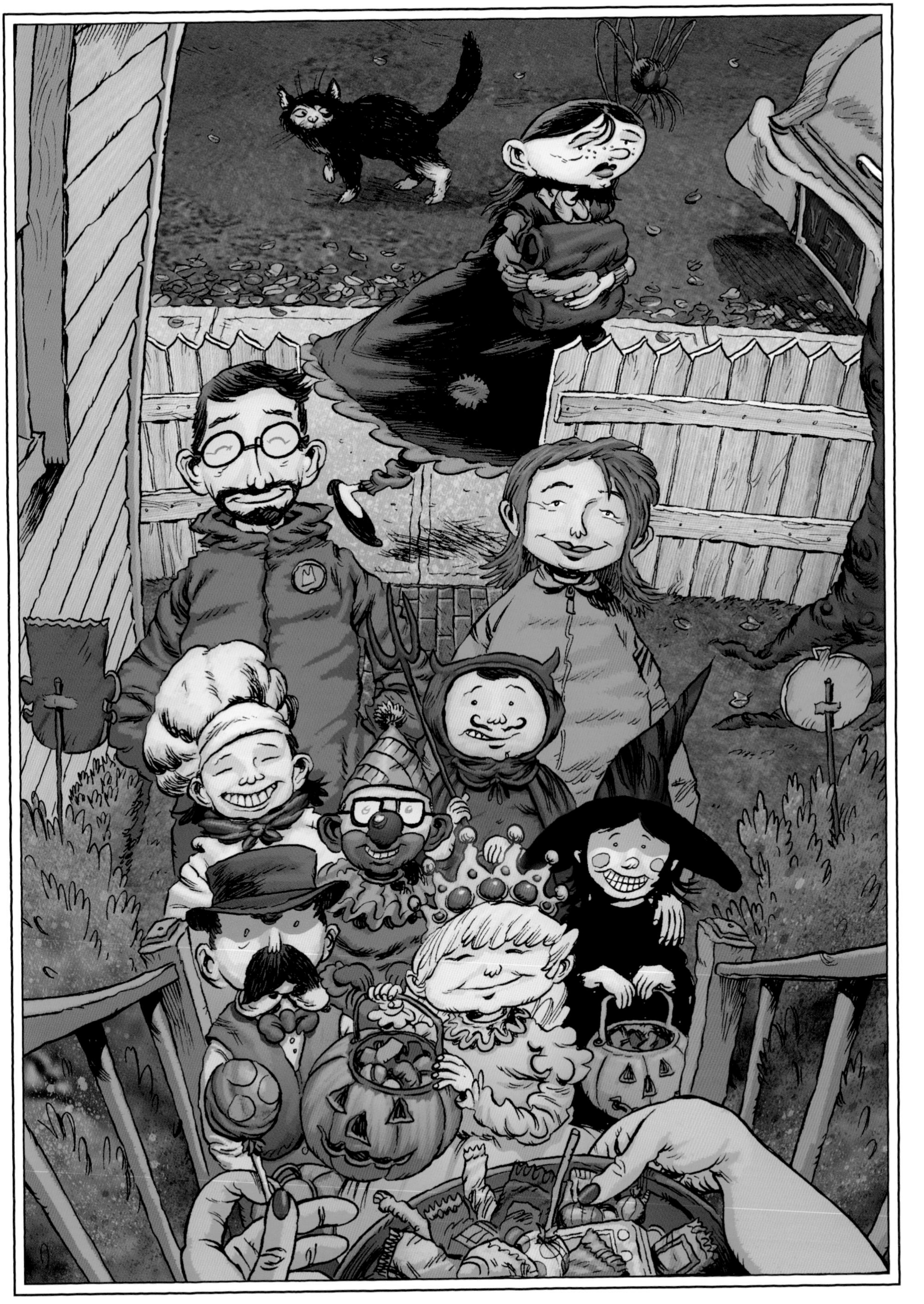

Later that night, Mary lay in her bed,
heart aching and breaking and filling with dread,
hugging her pillow with tears in her eyes,
for today was the day that her lows reached new highs.

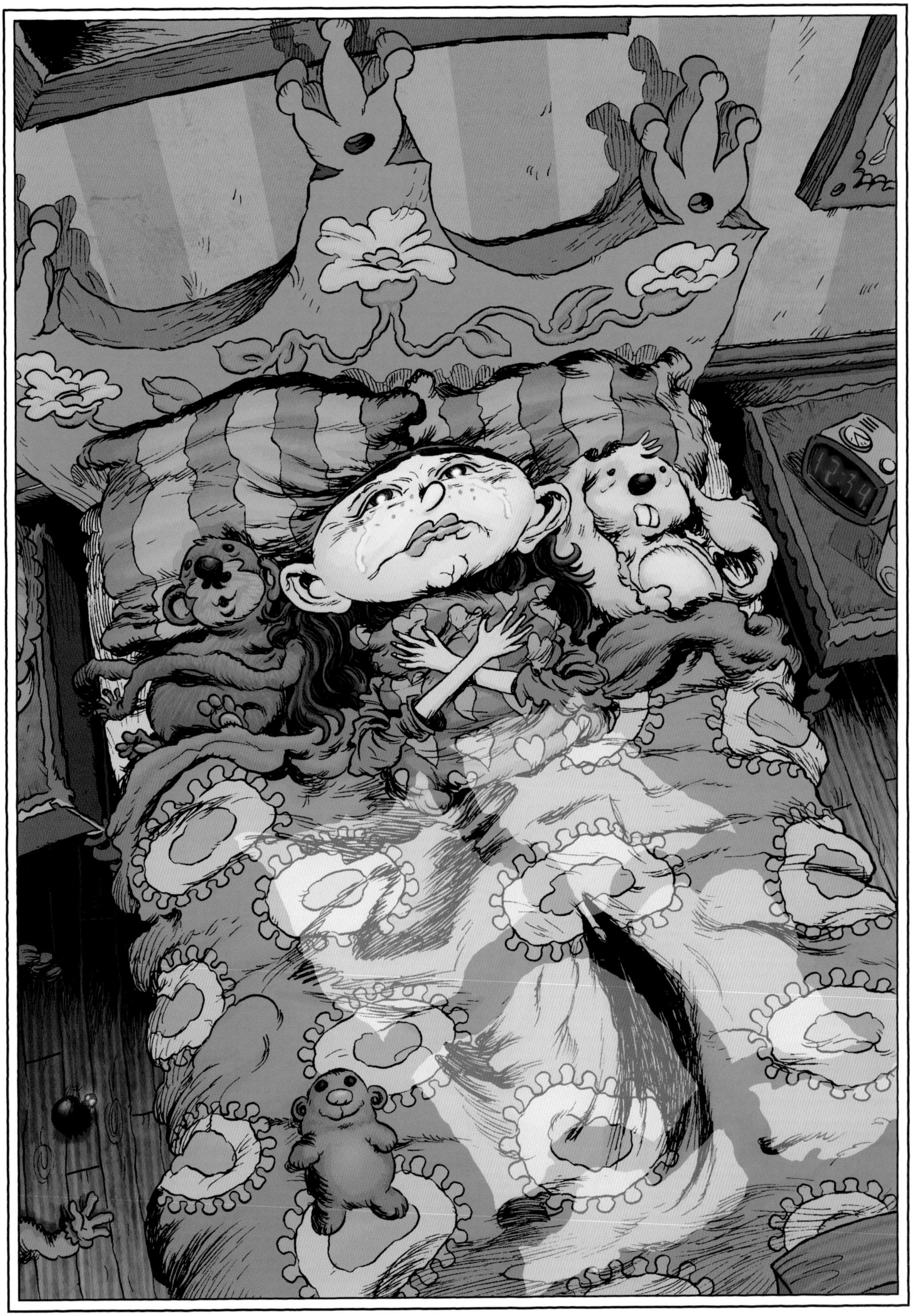
12:34

At thirteen past three Mary woke to a sound.

But who could have made it? No one else was around.

A bump, and a thump, then a thunderous BOOM!

as an odd little boy spilled out into the room.

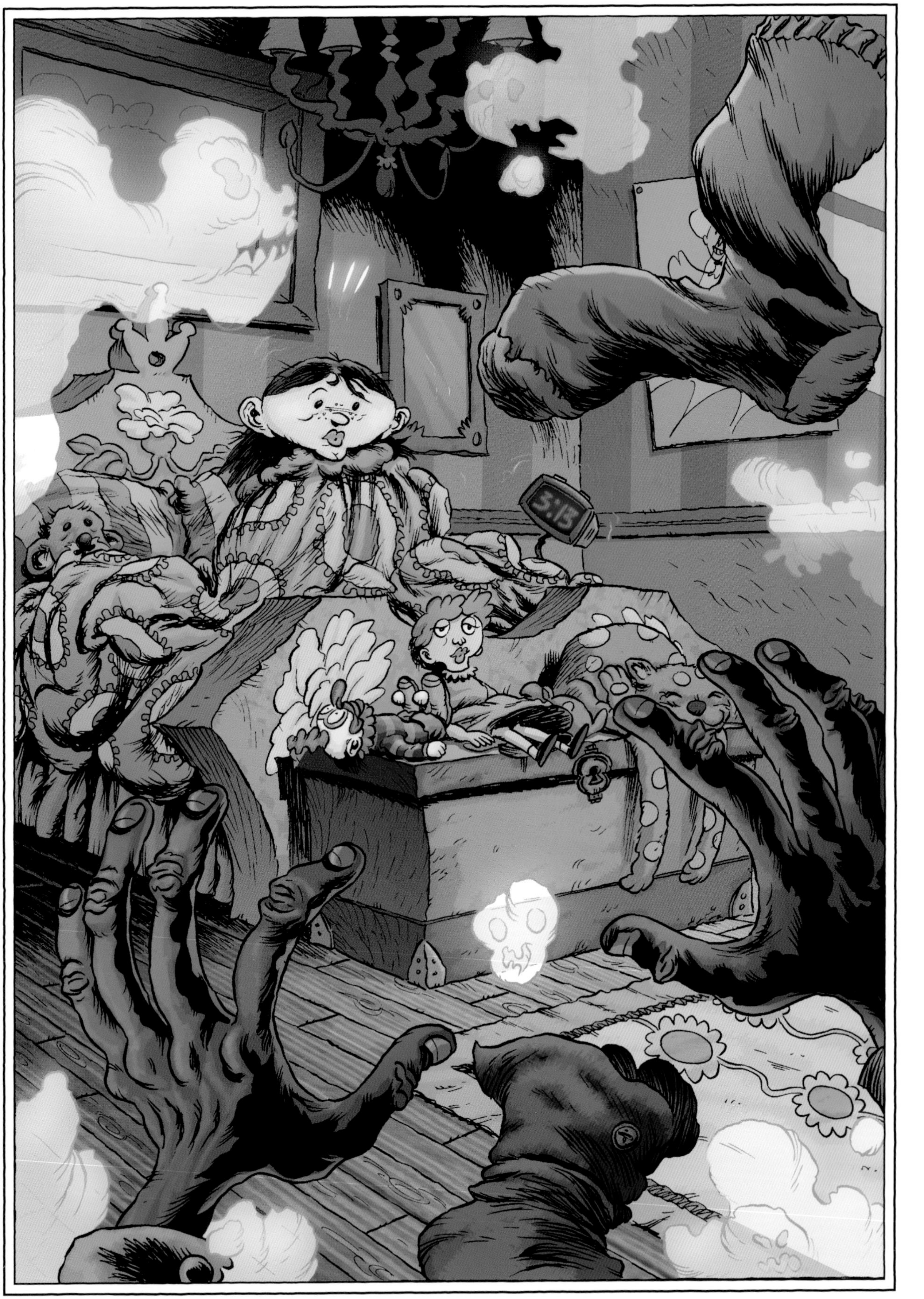
5:15

He managed a "BOO" as he fell to the floor,
having tripped on the lip of the rug by the door.
"The name's Edgar Grimm," the boy sadly said
and then sat next to Mary at the foot of her bed.

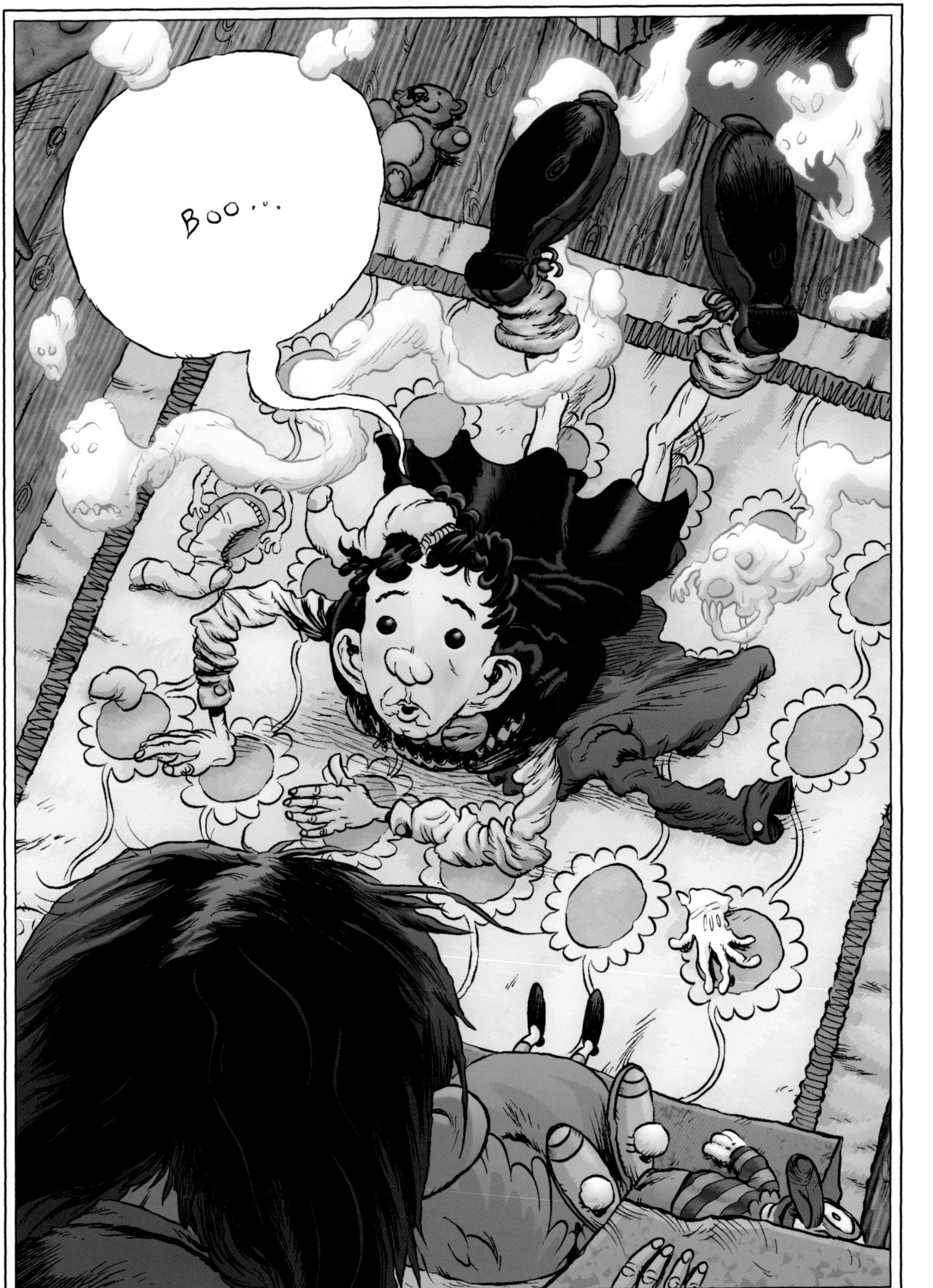
BOO...

I'm the son of the boogeyman, I'm supposed to be spooky.
But more times than not, I just come across kooky."
"That's funny," laughed Mary, and then volunteered,
"I'm supposed to be normal, but instead I'm just weird."

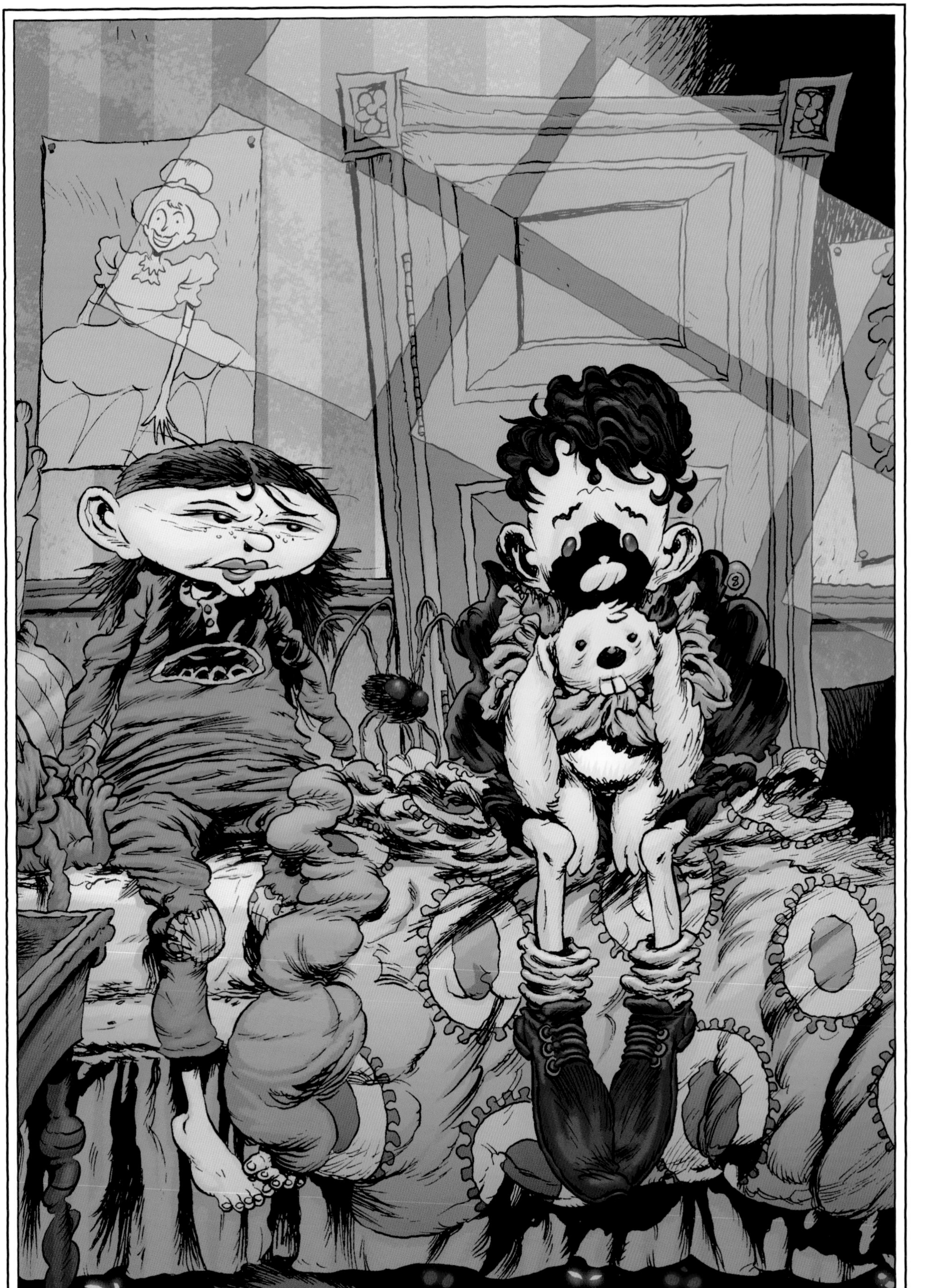

And so, just like that, without further ado
a bargain was struck between these unlikely two.
"I'll teach you," said Mary, "to be scary like me."
"In exchange," replied Ed, "I will make you scare-free."

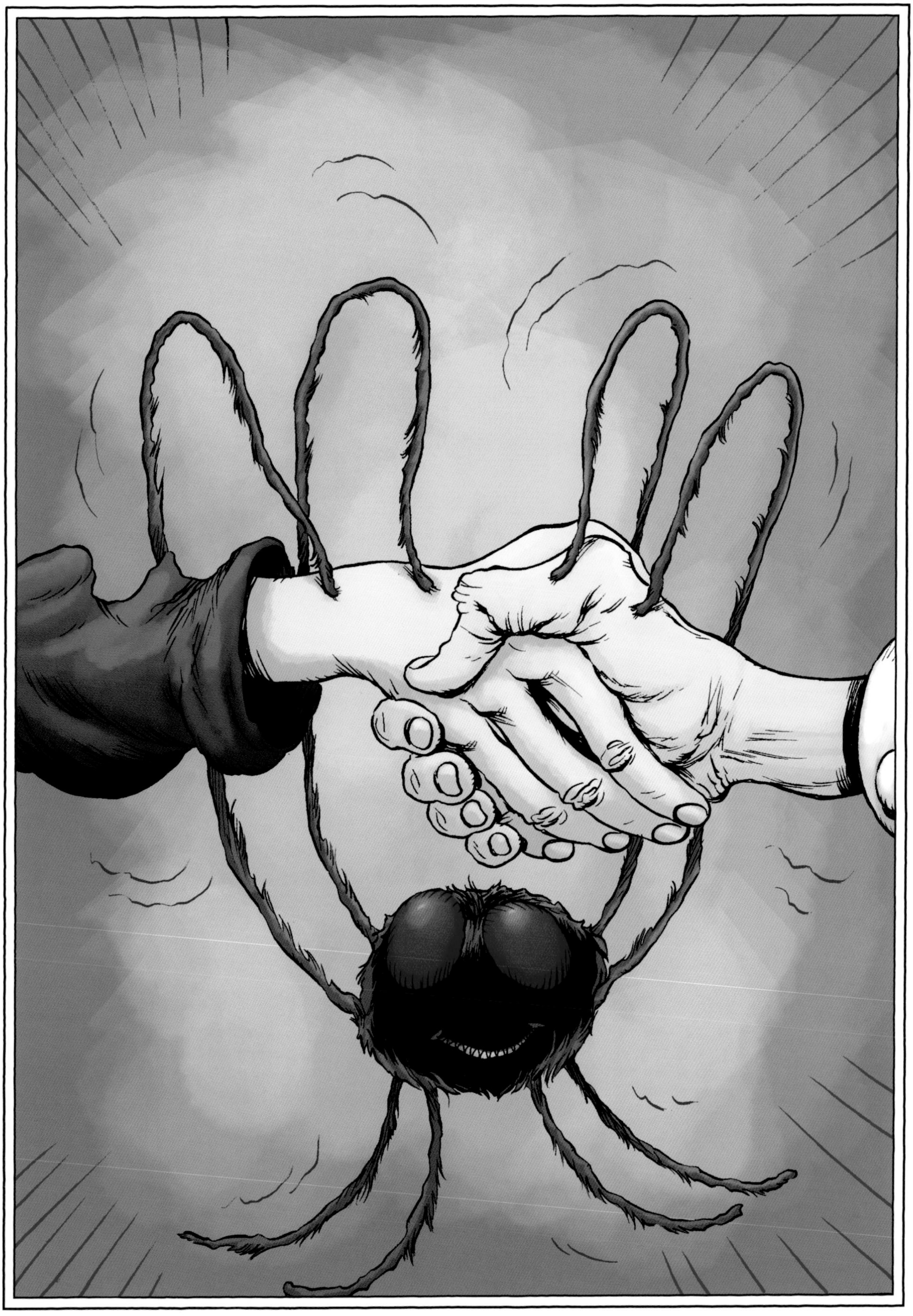

They started with basics; the clothes and the hair
which, in Mary's case, was no small affair.
"We'll fake a makeover to make you appear
like that which you aren't—a polite little dear."

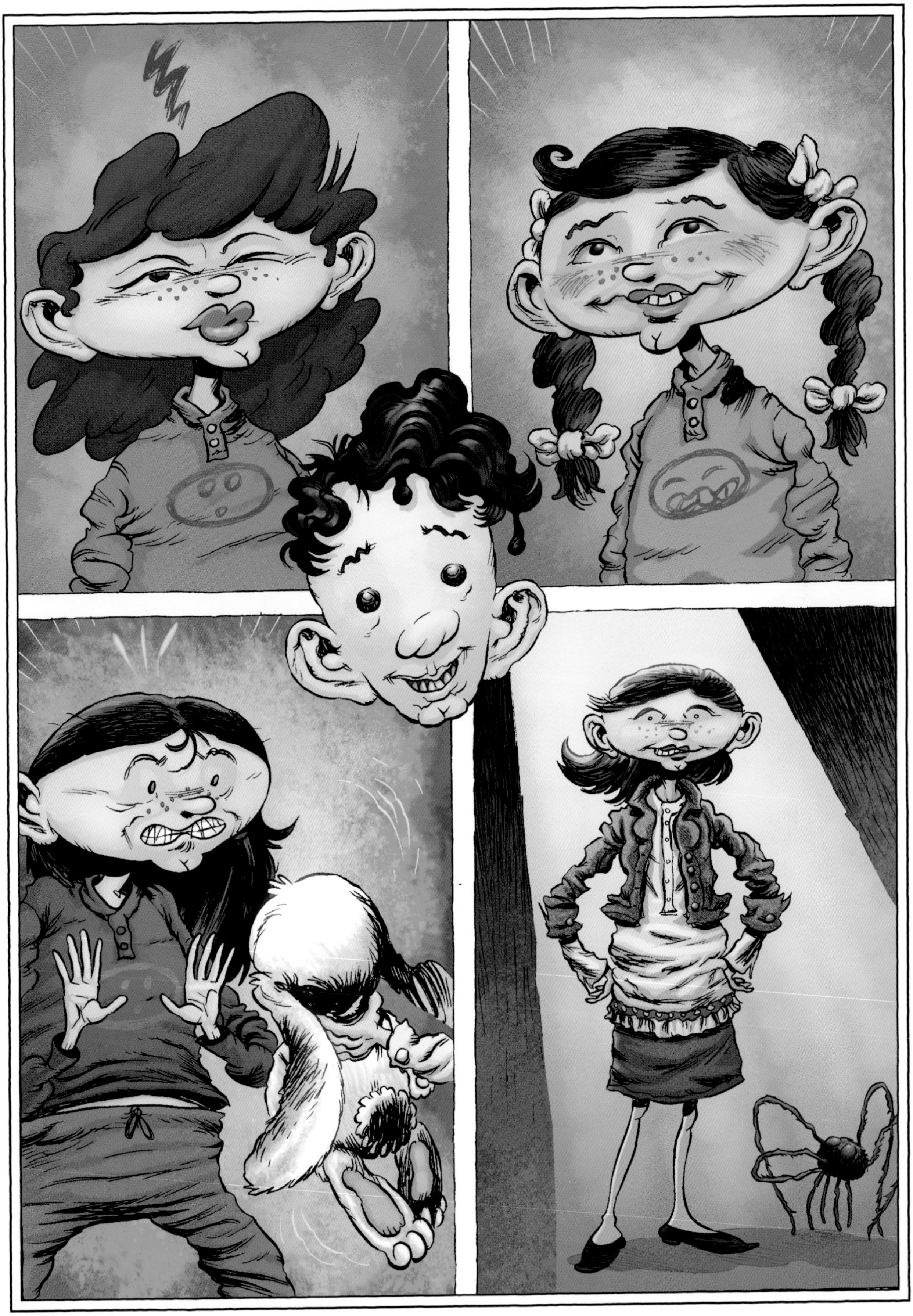

Then it was Ed's turn to learn a few tricks:
new faces, bad habits, strange noises, weird tics.
"Combined with a love for things squishy and odd
it should prove just enough to uphold the façade."

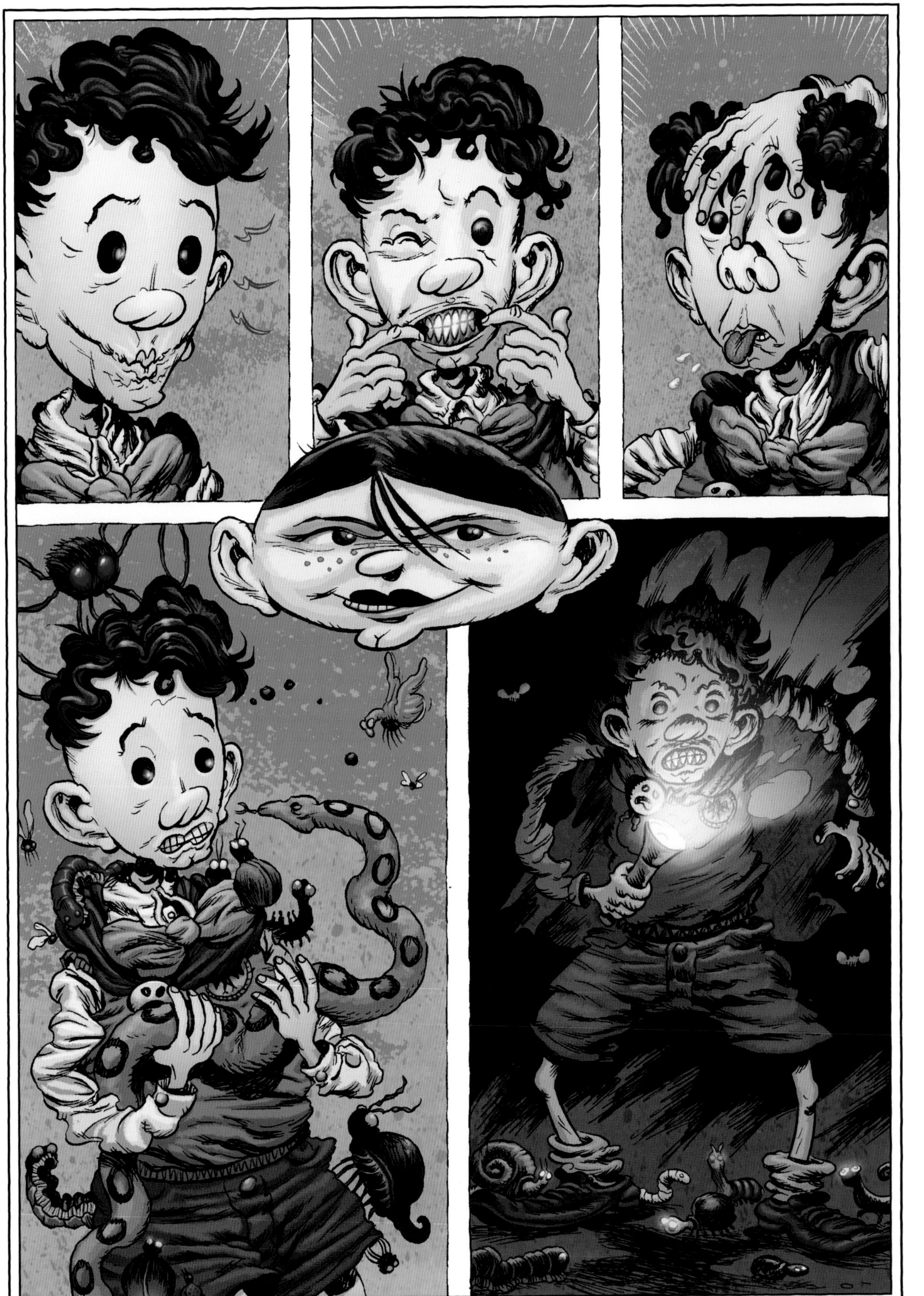

With that, the two children trekked into the night
to use their new gifts, to uplift and to fright.
Meanwhile, their parents discovered them gone,
and panicked with worry that something was wrong.

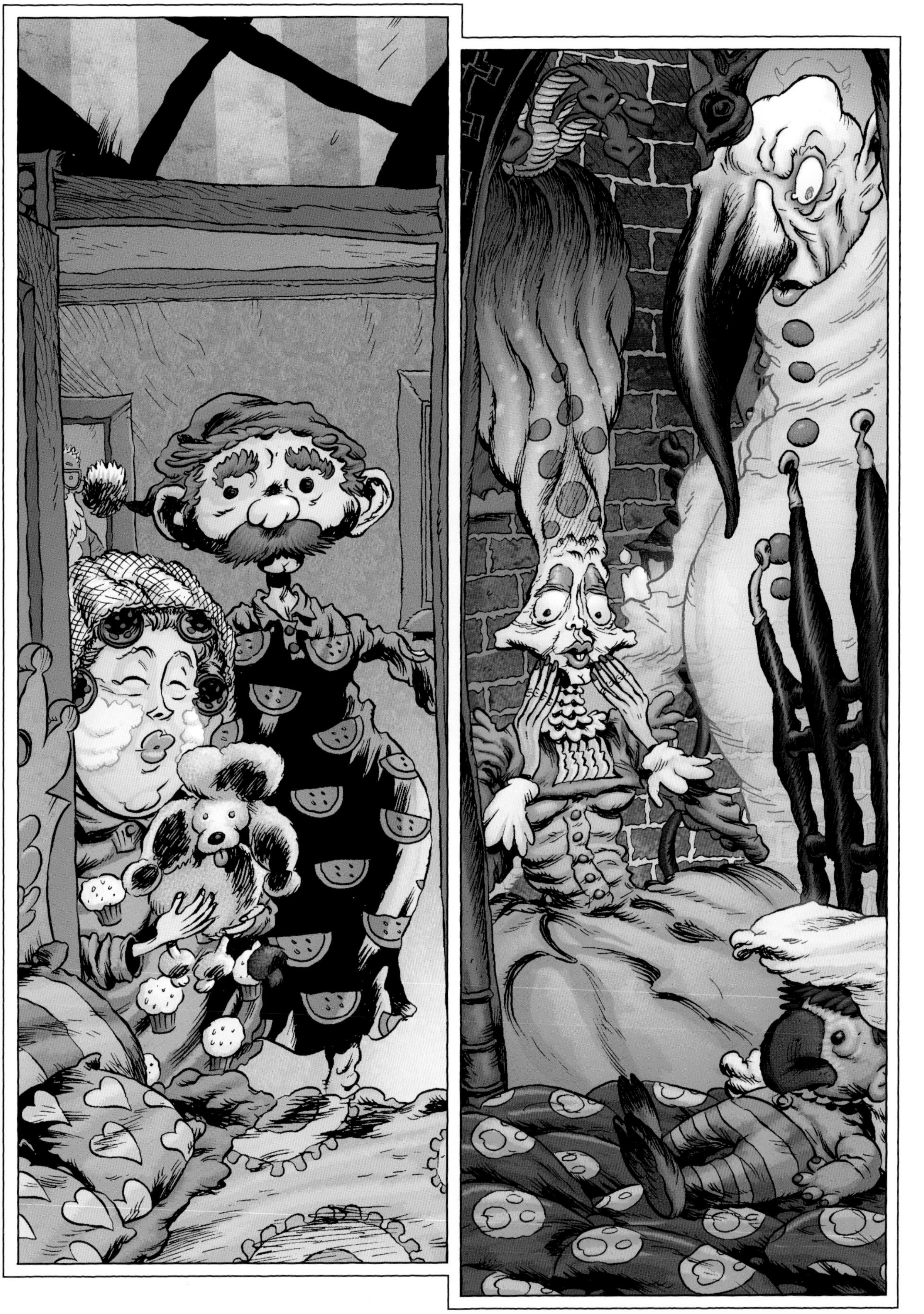

At that moment Edgar and Mary found out
they weren't the only ones hanging about.
A trio of Marys were tricking and treating,
while leaving behind a most unwelcome greeting.

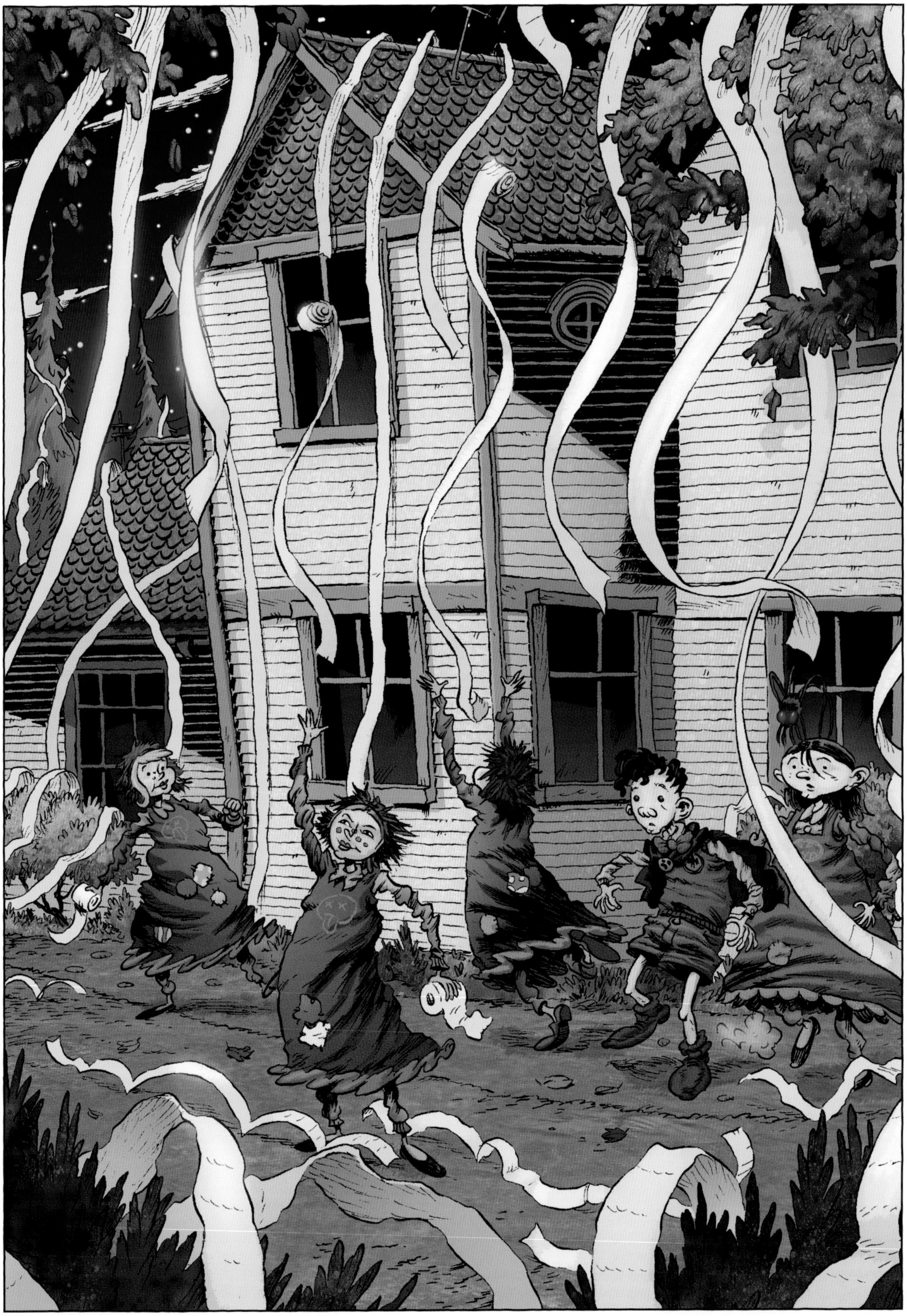

Now's your chance," Mary whispered. "Go scare them but good."
And with all he'd learned, Edgar thought that he could.
He made his worst face and then growled his worst growl!
But the girls started laughing, a cackling howl.

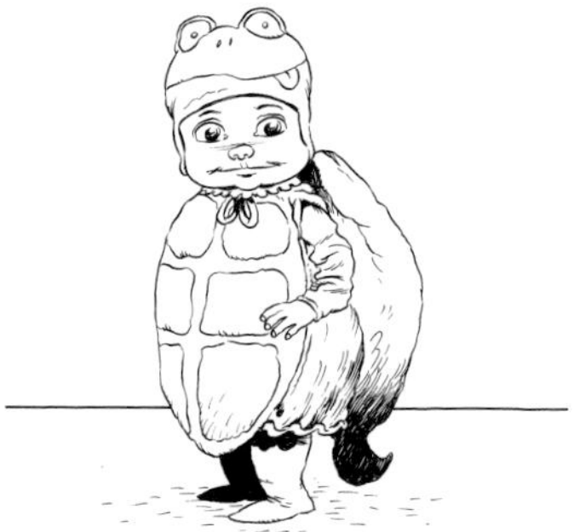

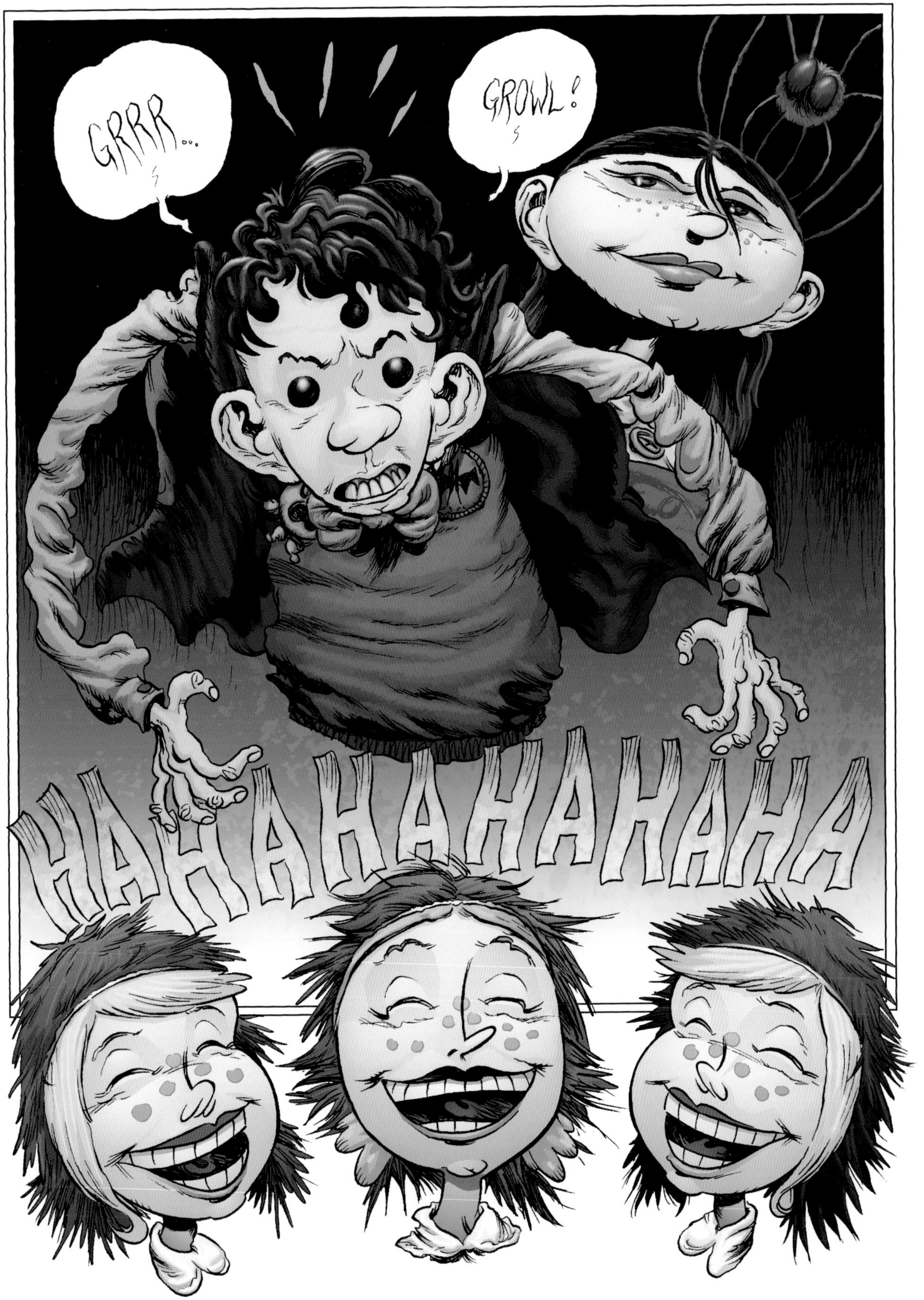
GRRR...
GROWL!
HAHAHAHAHAHAHA

That is, up until Edgar's parents arrived
and sent the girls screaming in fear for their lives.
They'd come for their son, not expecting to see
the one missing limb of their strange family tree.

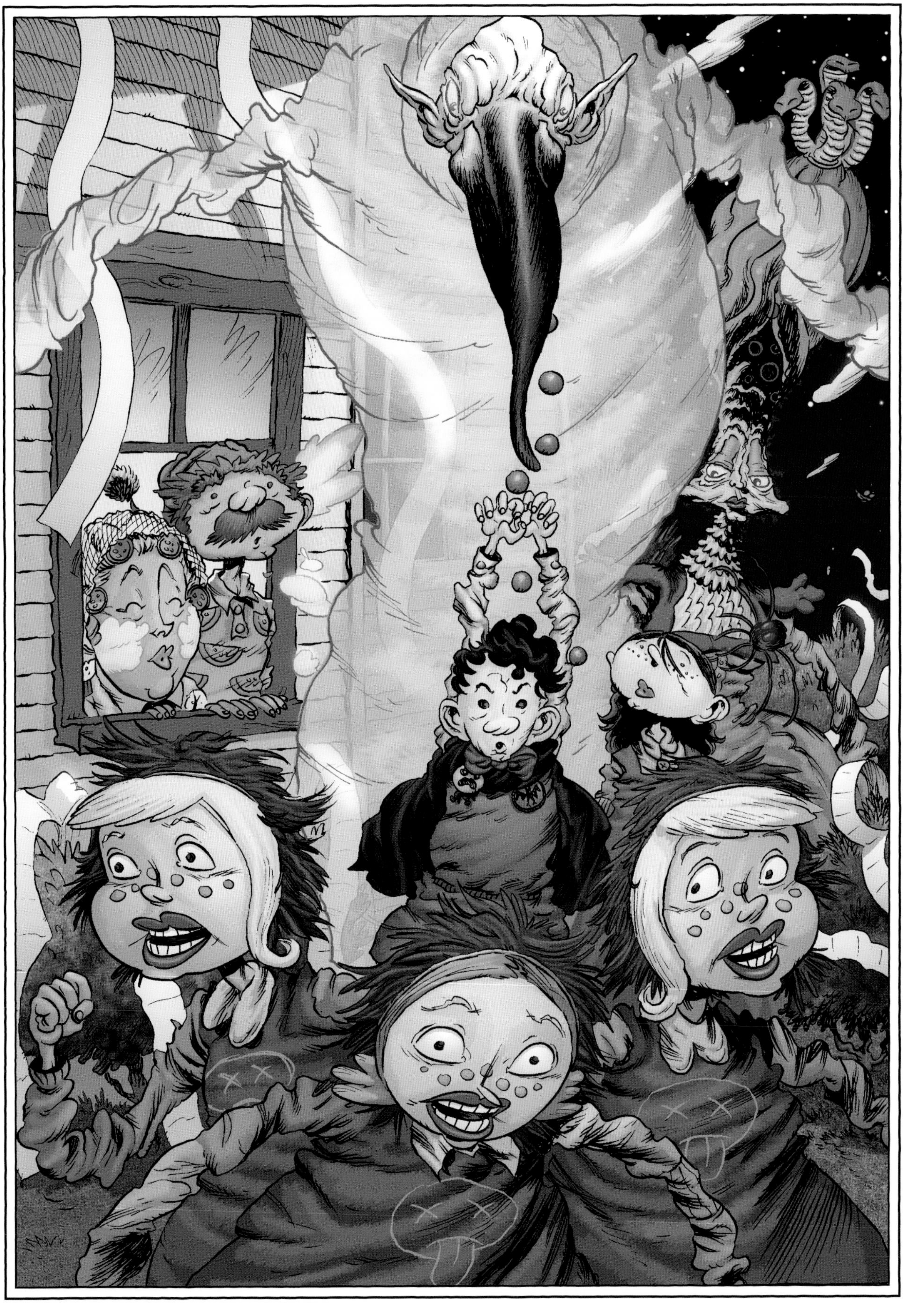

The resemblance quite simply could not be denied.

And as they embraced, full of joy, Mary cried . . .

"My whole life they told me I didn't belong.

Now I know, as you hold me, that they were all wrong."

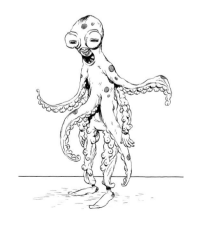

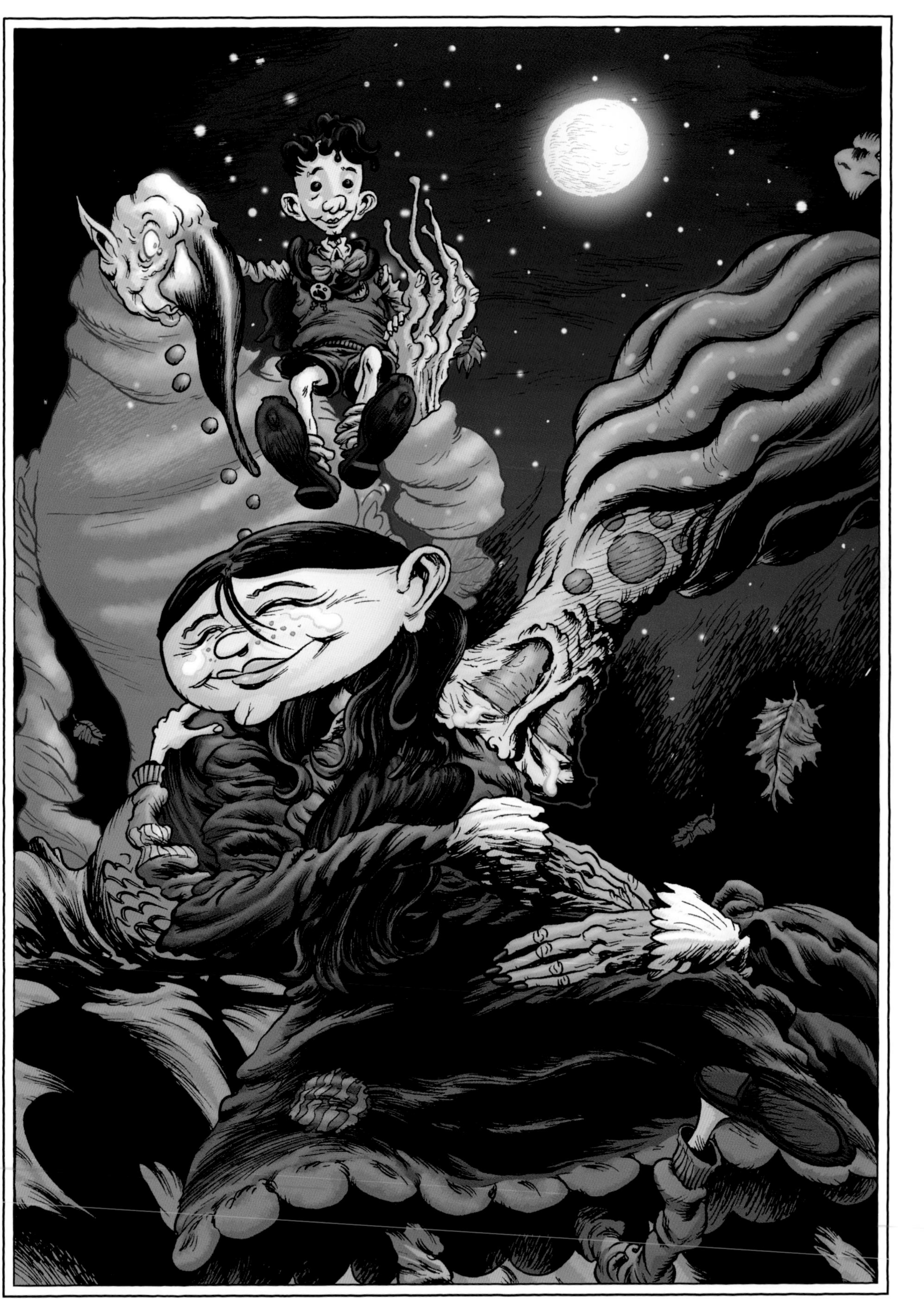

So Mary and Edgar were sister and brother
and the various parents all met one another.
A dysfunctional family, if ever there was
but they all made it work, 'cause that's what family does.